The policeman pu **arm. "Mr. Hastings, calm down."**

Lucas threw out his other arm, sending the paperwork scattering about the floor. He was caught in one of those stupid prank shows. Or something even worse. He had patients to see. He had notes to write up. He had no time for this. And the fact that the new colleague he'd considered attractive a few hours ago was in on this made it even more annoying.

"I have work to do," he declared.

There was an expletive from the floor at his feet. Skye was picking up the papers he had scattered, one clutched in her hand. She stood up, pushing her hair back from her face.

"I bet you do," she said. The tone of her voice stopped him dead.

The look on her face was stuck between incredulous, scornful and laughing. She held the paper before him. "Because if this is true—Lucas Hastings?" She said the word with a question in her voice. "You're the new Duke of Mercia, and a potential billionaire."

Dear Reader,

It's hard to believe that this is my fifty-first book for Harlequin. Time seems to have passed in a blink of an eye and I can still remember that day I got my call to tell me my first book—*It Started with a Pregnancy*—would be published. The fact that I'm still here shows you all how much fun I'm still having, so if any of you ever have a romance idea and think you might like to write a story, I urge you all to check out the Harlequin website and give it a go!

Cinderella's Kiss with the ER Doc is Skye and Lucas's story with some of my favourite themes. It's set around Christmas and New Year, and involves a surprise secret inheritance that reveals a title and a huge ancestral estate. Letting my characters work through their issues including bereavement, press interference and a self-centred relative before finally reaching their happy-ever-after was so much fun!

Hope you enjoy reading,

Scarlet Wilson

CINDERELLA'S KISS WITH THE ER DOC

SCARLET WILSON

HARLEQUIN
MEDICAL
ROMANCE

ⒽHARLEQUIN®
MEDICAL ROMANCE™

Recycling programs
for this product may
not exist in your area.

ISBN-13: 978-1-335-59517-1

Cinderella's Kiss with the ER Doc

Copyright © 2023 by Scarlet Wilson

Harlequin Enterprises ULC
22 Adelaide St. West, 41st Floor
Toronto, Ontario M5H 4E3, Canada
www.Harlequin.com

Printed in U.S.A.

Scarlet Wilson wrote her first story aged eight and has never stopped. She's worked in the health service for more than thirty years, having trained as a nurse and a health visitor. Scarlet now works in public health and lives on the west coast of Scotland with her fiancé and their two sons. Writing medical romances and contemporary romances is a dream come true for her.

Books by Scarlet Wilson

Harlequin Medical Romance

California Nurses
Nurse with a Billion Dollar Secret

Night Shift in Barcelona
The Night They Never Forgot

Neonatal Nurses
Neonatal Doc on Her Doorstep

A Festive Fling in Stockholm
His Blind Date Bride
Reawakened by the Italian Surgeon
Marriage Miracle in Emergency
Snowed In with the Surgeon
A Daddy for Her Twins

Visit the Author Profile page
at Harlequin.com for more titles.

To my team of girls: Elaine Kerr, Natalie McLeod, Jennifer Reid, Gillian Robertson and Ruth Convery. Is working supposed to be this much fun?

CHAPTER ONE

IT ONLY TOOK a few seconds for Skye Carter's Spidey-sense to start tingling. She'd been aware of the low-level tension in the air as she'd dashed between one cubicle and another. A quick scrub change had been required when an elderly patient had vomited on her, and she was pulling her blonde bob back into a scrunchie as she heard the voices escalate.

'He said he'd be back!' an angry man was shouting. 'And that was ten minutes ago.'

Her hair wouldn't comply with her wishes. It was her own fault. In a moment of odd impulse in the hairdresser's she'd asked her stylist to take three inches off her hair. The blonde bob was lovely but touched her shoulders, so didn't quite comply with nursing regulations, meaning she'd spent the last week battling with hair clips and scrunchies in an effort to tie it back.

She gave up and increased her strides as the shouting continued. 'Where on earth is he? This place is a disgrace. You should all be ashamed of yourselves.'

Skye took one glance at the whiteboard nearby to check the name of the patient.

Roan Parrish, three years old, Paeds.

A child. Of course. Relatives were always over-emotional when it was a child that was sick, and she didn't blame them one bit.

'Enough,' she said sharply as she stepped into the cubicle and turned to look at the red-faced man. 'I'm Skye Carter, the A&E sister. What can I do to help you?'

Some people would question her de-escalation technique. But over the years Skye had learned not to go in with a quiet, nice approach. She'd realised when someone was loud, angry and potentially aggressive, to draw a line in the sand straight away. It tended to jerk back people's immediate behaviour, and let them know she wasn't going to be bullied. She certainly wasn't going to put up with bad behaviour towards her staff, but going on to ask how she could help tended to cut straight to the heart of the problem, where people could say exactly what it was they wanted.

The man gave a few short blinks and pointed at the child on the bed. 'He said he was going to be back soon.'

'Who said that?' She picked up the nearest chart to scan what it said. Another glance back at the board told her that although the child had been assigned to Paediatrics, they hadn't yet attended. Great.

'The doctor who was here. Scottish guy.'

She nodded, glancing at a few more notes. Lucas Hastings. She hadn't met him yet as she'd been on leave for a while—but, to be fair, she'd heard good things. He was a new registrar in the A&E department and at his level she would have expected him to have dealt with this child appropriately.

She moved over to Roan, who was lying on the bed with his eyes closed, his dark skin damp. A quick touch of his forehead told her he was running a slight temperature. He was attached to a monitor, so she pressed the button to check his blood pressure again and recorded his readings, pulling an ear thermometer from a drawer to add to the information already gathered.

There was a thudding noise outside and a

guy appeared at the curtains, breathless and carrying a unit of blood in his hand. His brow furrowed as he looked at Skye but, seeing her uniform, he carried on into the cubicle and started to speak quickly.

'Mr Parrish, sorry for the delay, but the lab called me. Roan's blood levels are a concern and we need to start a transfusion as soon as possible.'

It took Skye's brain a few seconds to adjust. The doctor had a thick Scottish burr, and his words came out quickly. She could see something similar happening with Mr Parrish. The man blinked and opened his mouth, but no words came out.

Skye blinked too. Lucas Hastings was more than handsome. Tall, broad-shouldered, with slightly longer dark hair and eyes the colour of an emerald ring she'd once admired in a jeweller's shop. At twenty thousand pounds, it was the kind of thing a girl could only dream of.

Lucas put his hand on the man's upper arm. 'Is there any way to get in touch with Roan's parents? I'd really like to talk to them too.'

Skye moved around behind them and grabbed an IV infusion kit and infusion pump. Her actions were instinctive and automatic. It only took her a few seconds to set them up and run the blood through the line.

This guy wasn't the parent? No wonder he was so worried. She gave him a quick glance. Mr Parrish wore his years well. He could be anything from early fifties to late sixties, and in this day and age it didn't pay to assume anything about who might be a parent.

Mr Parrish shook his head. 'My son and his wife are in the Caribbean. She's from there, and her sister is getting married today. They're only away for four days and Roan is staying with me.'

Lucas gave a nod. 'Was Roan born here?'

Skye tilted her head. Her years of experience meant she knew exactly why Lucas was asking the question. It was smart. But not all doctors got there quite so quickly.

Mr Parrish shook his head. 'No, he was born in Africa. My son was working there at the time. We have family there, and he was helping set up the accounts for the family business.'

'I don't suppose you know if Roan had a heel prick test as a baby?'

Skye could tell Mr Parrish was starting to get agitated again. He shook his head and tugged at the collar of his polo shirt. 'I have no idea. Does it matter?'

Skye handed over the electronic prescribing tablet to Lucas, indicating to him to prescribe the blood transfusion. It couldn't be set up until it was prescribed and they'd both double-checked the labelling. Experience had told her exactly where this conversation was heading.

'Have a seat, Mr Parrish,' she said gently.

'Is it bad?' His dark eyes were full of anguish as he turned towards her. Skye's stomach twisted. He was terrified for his grandson.

'It's manageable,' she replied. She was always completely honest with her patients.

Lucas's green eyes met hers. She'd never worked with this guy before, and had no idea about his patient skills or techniques. But somehow he seemed like a safe pair of hands.

He looked as if he might want to say something to her, but instead his fingers moved quickly over the prescribing tablet, then set it down next to Mr Parrish. He took a breath. 'Have you heard of sickle cell disease?'

The man's nose and brow wrinkled. He gave a slow nod but still had a look of confusion on his face. That told Skye a lot. He clearly didn't have someone in his family already affected by this disease.

Lucas continued. 'Our tests show that Roan has sickle cell disease. In the UK, all new babies are checked with a heel prick test after they are born. Because Roan was born in Africa, it's likely he missed that. It would have picked up the fact that Roan might be affected by sickle cell disease. It's why the lab phoned me, and I went to get the blood.'

Mr Parrish pulled out his phone. His hands were shaking. 'Is this going to help my grandson?'

Lucas nodded. 'We'll get him started on treatment. I'm really sorry the paediatricians haven't seen him yet. But this can't wait. We'll start this now, and I can give you a basic outline.'

Mr Parrish shook his head. He was still fumbling with his phone and Skye put her hand on his shoulder. 'Is it your son you want to get hold of?'

He nodded and she closed her hand over his. 'Would you like me to do it for you?'

His bottom lip trembled and he nodded again.

She waited until he slid the phone open, then glanced at Roan's electronic record for his dad's name. She dabbed her initials into the electronic prescribing tablet, gestured for Lucas to do the same and held the blood label where they could both check it.

She read the details out loud, waited for him to confirm, then also confirmed the run rate for the IV infusion. Within seconds, it was set up and running.

She gave them both a smile. 'Mr Parrish, I'll step outside and speak to your son.'

She just knew that he wasn't going to be in a position to absorb anything she told him right now. So she found the number, adjusted the dialling code to connect with the Caribbean and took a deep breath.

After a few seconds of hesitation, the call connected and was answered after a few long rings, to sounds of music. 'Dad?' came the yell.

'Sean Parrish? My name is Skye Carter. I'm a sister at A&E in The Harlington Hospital, London.'

It took Lucas five attempts to find the new mystery sister. He tried the nurses' station, the treatment room, the office, the sluice and then the linen closet before he was finally pointed in the direction of the staffroom. It could be hard to find a quiet space in one of the busiest A&Es in London.

As he pushed the door open he could hear her talking calmly. She was explaining in clear terms what sickle cell disease was, how they were currently treating Roan and what the paediatricians would do next. This clearly wasn't her first rodeo, and he was impressed by her knowledge of something that wouldn't be routine in A&E.

He waited until she'd ended the call before he picked up a packet of biscuits and sat down next to her, passing them to her. 'Thanks for that.'

She picked out the top digestive and took a bite. 'No problem. Is someone with Mr Parrish right now?'

He nodded. 'One of your staff, Leona, is keeping an eye on Roan's obs and sitting with Mr Parrish. The paed has just arrived. They had an arrest. That's why they were so long.'

Skye's eyebrows raised. 'In Paeds? Everything okay?'

Lucas leaned back against the slightly battered chair. 'Severe allergic reaction. Transferred to PICU on an adrenaline infusion.'

They both sat for a few moments. No one

liked it when kids were sick. An arrest in an adult was difficult enough, but in a child?

He held out his hand. 'Lucas Hastings,' he said. 'I've been here a few months. I don't think we've met before.'

'I haven't been here,' she said quickly, before sliding her hand into his. 'Skye Carter.'

She didn't expand on why she hadn't been there, and even though he was curious he wasn't going to ask. Her warm hand felt good in his and she had a firm grip that she pulled away a little quicker than he hoped for.

'Where did you work before, Lucas?'

'Liverpool, Glasgow, and a short spell in East Anglia with the air ambulance service.'

That seemed to catch her attention and she frowned. 'How did you land that?'

'A friend was sick at short notice,' he said. 'He asked me to cover and it suited them, and me.'

She took another bite of her biscuit. 'Good experience.' She gave an approving nod.

He pulled a face. 'Yes, and no. Sea and mountain rescue were certainly interesting. A lot of farming accidents. But the worst part was always being first on scene at some of the country road traffic accidents.'

She closed her eyes for a second and he

could see her shudder. If she'd worked here a while, she'd likely seen just as many horrors as he had. He was trying to figure this new colleague out.

It had been a surprise to sprint back into the hospital cubicle and see the unfamiliar blonde, holding her own with an air of authority. Her swift movements and how she'd just spoken to Roan Parrish's dad told him that she had experience that matched his own. He was curious about her. Skye? The staff here were friendly enough but no one had mentioned a missing sister.

'Cool accent,' she said unexpectedly. 'Which part of Scotland are you from?'

He gave a brief laugh. 'All of it, and none of it.' Her nose wrinkled and he continued. 'I was born somewhere near London, but then my mum moved to Dumfries. We stayed in Glasgow, Ayrshire, Edinburgh, even the Shetland Islands at one point, then we moved to Europe for a while. Spain, Gibraltar and Portugal, before coming back to Scotland so I could finish secondary school.'

Skye gave a wide smile. 'Wow, what a childhood.' There was a wistful light in her eyes. 'It's been London and London for me, and I always wanted to try someplace else.'

'Another country?'

She shrugged. 'Maybe. Or even another part of this country.' She took a breath and her smile tightened a little. 'I had family ties so had to stay put, but that's changed now, so it might be time for a change.' Her eyes looked off to the far wall, and he could tell she was seeing images in her mind. 'Where's your mum now?' she asked, the smile reappearing.

He got the oddest sense of vulnerability from her. Family ties that had changed? It was clear she was trying to change the subject and he understood that.

He said the words he'd said a number of times before. 'Not actually sure right now. Let's just say she's always been a bit of a wanderer.'

Skye gave him an odd look. 'Don't you keep in touch?'

'I try to,' he said, instantly knowing that Skye would pick up the implication. 'She's an independent woman, always moving onto the next place, and the next circle of friends. My friends at university nicknamed her the Scarlet Pimpernel.'

Skye let out a laugh. 'What do you mean?'

'You know the phrase: *They seek him here, they seek him there*...? My mum is a bit like that. I never know where she will pop up next.' He smiled as he remembered the late-night calls declaring she was in a part of the world that he'd sometimes never even heard of.

Skye took the last bite of her biscuit. 'Straight over my head. Guess I'm not cultured enough. We didn't do *The Scarlet Pimpernel* at school. We did *Romeo and Juliet* and I had definite issues with it.'

Lucas raised his eyebrows and felt a little spark of...something. He couldn't remember the last time he'd enjoyed a conversation like this. In theory, he'd always said he wouldn't date a colleague, but maybe it was time to reconsider?

He folded his arms and prayed his pager wouldn't sound any second. 'What were your issues?'

She threw up her hands. 'Where to start? Their age. The lies. The drama. Why are fifty per cent of all stories just about people not talking to each other and being truthful? They knew each other for a day. Young as she is, Juliet is on the rebound. And Romeo wasn't really romantic, more like—' she lifted her fingers into the air '—creepy.'

Lucas started to laugh. 'A million teenage hearts are breaking all over the world right now.'

Skye raised her eyebrows, giving him a clear view of her bright blue eyes, which exactly matched her scrubs. 'Fools.'

The door opened behind them and one of the other staff members gave them a quick glance. 'Can you two cover Resus? Ambulance on the way with an older man who's been attacked and is apparently in a bad way.'

They were on their feet in seconds, no hesitation, just a quick march down the corridor, where Skye washed her hands and donned a plastic apron. As she moved aside to make way for Lucas, she had a quick check over the equipment. She couldn't deny her sense of pride in her staff. Even after a few major incidents in Resus today, everything was restocked and in place, exactly as it should be.

She'd missed the familiar surroundings, and the familiar faces. She'd missed hearing the stories of teenage sons or baby granddaughters. Of Vixen the very wicked cat, or Albus, the not too bright sausage dog, belonging to one of her staff. For the last seven years this place and these people had been like an extended family to her.

Coming back hadn't been difficult. But her future thoughts might be. The rush of London was dulling. The Saturday night drunks and stabbings were certainly wearing her down. From the moment Skye Carter had her first nurse placement in A&E she'd known it was the place for her. But now? She was beginning to wonder what else might be out there. There was nothing to limit nurses these days, from advanced practice to specialisms. Skye just had to decide what direction she wanted to go in.

The approaching sound of a siren drew both her and Lucas to the receiving doors of the A&E unit. As the ambulance backed up, Lucas opened the back doors and Skye saw a familiar face.

'What you got, Nalin?'

Her Sri Lankan friend looked up and his face broke into a wide smile as he manoeuvred the stretcher towards them both. 'How's my favourite A&E sister?'

'Good.' She nodded as the wheels of the stretcher dropped down as it glided from the ambulance.

The other paramedic strolled round from the front of the ambulance and slung an arm around her shoulder, dropping a quick kiss on her head. 'Great to see you back, Skye.'

'Thanks, Jim.'

Her heart swelled. Both were good friends, and she knew their sentiments were entirely genuine. Over the years they'd seen some sights together, from major road traffic accidents, building collapses and train collisions. She'd trust these men with her life, and even though only a few seconds had passed she could sense the curious gaze from Lucas.

Nalin started talking. 'This is Albert Cunningham. Eighty-one. We think he was mugged and attacked, then run over by a car.'

Skye winced as she fell into step beside the stretcher as they wheeled it inside, her eyes on the portable monitor. 'Bad day,' she said quietly.

Nalin continued. 'We suspect a left fractured femur, with possible tib and fib fractures too. Head injury, Glasgow Coma Scale four at present. Rib injuries. Possible internal injuries too. BP is low at ninety over sixty, tachycardic at one hundred and forty. Only thing normal is his temperature.' As they pushed him into Resus, Nalin gave a sad sigh. 'He hasn't been conscious at all since we reached him.' He handed over a chart. 'At this point, know that we haven't given him any analgesics so far and I imagine he's going to need some.'

'Police been called?' asked Lucas.

Jim nodded. 'They were at the scene and are following us in. They have his personal effects.'

'Who would do this to an old guy?' Skye sighed as she looked down at him. The over-coat he was wearing was thick and elegant, the suit underneath probably from a Savile Row tailor, and the leather shoes on his feet had likely been handcrafted. Like a number of people in London, this man was well dressed. She was likely going to have to cut off clothes that cost more than she earned in a few months.

Lucas continued his examination as Skye slid the man's arm out of his coat and drew some blood from the crook of his elbow.

'Mr Cunningham?' She spoke gently but there was no response.

Two dark figures appeared at the door and Skye recognised one. 'Hi, Laura,' she said, and smiled.

'Skye, you're back. Nice to see you.' The

police sergeant was carrying a large bag with a number of items and was wearing a pair of gloves. 'I see you've got Mr Cunningham.'

The two paramedics were retrieving their equipment and getting ready to leave.

Lucas looked up and gave a nod. 'We have. I haven't finished assessing him yet.'

He recorded something in the notes and then looked up again. 'Apologies, we haven't met before. I'm Lucas Hastings.'

The two officers exchanged glances. Laura took a moment to answer. She flipped open her notebook and turned it to face Lucas. 'This Lucas Hastings?'

He glanced at the page and pulled back. 'That's my date of birth and address—what's going on?'

There was a deep furrow in his brow, just as Mr Cunningham gave a little twitch. Skye leaned over him quickly to reassess his neuro obs as the phone beside her rang. Her thoughts were spinning. What on earth was going on? Why had the police turned up here, looking for Lucas? It was more than a little unusual, but she didn't want to start asking questions. She had a patient to take care of, one who might be deteriorating rapidly.

Neither of their police colleagues had a

chance to reply before Lucas answered the phone and said a few short words. 'CT scan is ready for us.' He looked at Skye as Mr Cunningham gave a little twitch again. She was leaning over the patient checking the pupils of his eyes with a pen torch. 'We'll have to go with him. He's too unstable. I'm worried he's going to seize.'

The police exchanged glances. 'What does that mean?'

Skye started unplugging things and moving the monitor onto the edge of the patient trolley. 'It means that Mr Cunningham might have a blood clot on his brain, caused by his injuries, that might cause him to seize. He's starting to show signs. We need him scanned and may need to relieve the pressure on his brain.'

She turned around and opened a few drawers and took some sealed sterile surgical equipment from them.

'Good thinking,' murmured Lucas.

He turned to a healthcare support worker who'd just come into the room. 'We're taking this man to CT. Can you phone Neuro and ask them for an urgent consult? If they can, I'd appreciate it if they can meet us there.'

The healthcare support worker looked at

the name on the tablet Lucas handed him and gave a nod. 'No problem.'

As Lucas and Skye started wheeling the patient trolley down the corridor, Lucas looked over his shoulder towards the police. 'If you still need to speak to me, you'd better come with us.'

Lucas's stomach was knotted as they walked swiftly down the corridor. He wasn't a criminal. He knew he hadn't done anything wrong. So why on earth were there two police colleagues in his A&E department, with a notebook with his details in it?

As far as he was aware, he didn't even have an outstanding parking ticket. He started to think about the traffic around London. Had he unwittingly gone in a lane meant only for either buses or taxis? Had he missed a traffic light? Had he been caught speeding?

Lucas was generally a careful driver. He didn't even drive that often in London, making it even more unlikely. But he couldn't think of another reason for the police to be looking for him. Some unknown traffic infringement was his best guess.

The CT staff were ready for them, and assisted in moving Mr Cunningham into position for the scan.

Lucas, Skye and the two accompanying police officers moved into the viewing room while the scan was taking place. Lucas's eyes were fixed on the screen, suspecting what he might see.

'Who would do this to an old man?' murmured Skye before turning to face the officers. 'Where did you find him, Laura?'

Laura paused before answering. 'Just a few streets away, actually.'

Skye frowned. The hospital didn't have a huge car park as it was in the middle of London, and staff and visitors did sometimes park in the streets round about.

'Was he coming to visit someone?'

'Yes and no,' replied Laura, before casting her eyes in Lucas's direction.

Lucas almost felt her gaze on him. He looked up for a few seconds, shaking his head. 'I don't know him.'

The other officer started speaking. 'We think he was robbed because of his car. Apparently, it's an Aston Martin.'

'Like James Bond?' said Lucas, because that was what he generally associated Aston Martins with.

'More than you know,' replied the officer. 'It was actually his car that was used in one of the films a few years ago.'

'No way,' said Skye, her eyes going between the officers and the scanning screen.

Laura nodded. 'Someone saw the same car speeding away. We suspect he also had a watch and wallet stolen.'

Now Lucas was curious. 'So, if his wallet was stolen, how did you work out who he was so quickly?'

Laura held up a briefcase. 'There was nothing of value in here. Only paperwork. But that's why we're coming to you, Lucas.'

Now, he was thoroughly confused. 'What are you talking about?' As soon as the words were out of his mouth he held up his hand, recognising something on the screen. 'Large subdural haematoma,' he said quickly. As he reached for the phone, a woman in a white coat walked in.

'What have you got for me?' she asked, then glanced at the screen. 'Oh, dear.'

Skye gave a nod towards the officers. 'This is our neurosurgeon, Aasa Sangha.'

Aasa gave a quick glance and raised her eyebrows as Lucas handed her an electronic tablet with all the patient details.

'He's just been admitted after a robbery and assault. Left fractured femur. Tib and fib fractures too. There may be other internal injuries as he was also run over, but we prioritised the head scan due to his GCS reading.'

Aasa nodded. 'I have to relieve the pressure now.' She glanced at the tablet, then at the police officers. 'Do you have next of kin details or are there relatives here?'

Both shook their head. 'Still attempting to find a next of kin.'

Aasa turned to Skye and Lucas. 'In that case, I'm going to take Mr Cunningham straight to surgery. I'll be in touch once surgery is complete and—' she looked at his chart again '—I'll talk to one of the orthopods about the bone injuries.'

Lucas gave a grateful nod. In other circumstances he might have needed to do an emergency burr hole in Mr Cunningham's skull. Thankfully, that was not tonight. As Aasa asked some staff members to assist her and set off towards the theatre, Lucas was left with the distinct feeling that he was currently under the microscope.

He wanted to get back to A&E and continue to see patients.

'You still haven't explained why you're here,' he said bluntly to the two officers.

Laura set down the briefcase and flipped it open, lifting out a stack of papers. 'We haven't had a chance to look at these properly. But Mr Cunningham had your name and place of work in his possession. When we opened his briefcase we found this.' She handed over a large envelope.

If Lucas had been confused before, its contents didn't help.

The Last Will and Testament of Ralph Ignatius Cornwell Hastings, Duke of Mercia.

'Who is this?' he asked. 'And where's Mercia? Is it European? Like Monaco?'

Laura bit her bottom lip and took a deep breath. 'Turn the page.'

Lucas flipped over the page and his eyes scanned the legal jargon that no one understood. He stopped reading at the *only son* point.

He murmured the words out loud. 'Only son, Lucas Harrington Hastings.' He looked up. 'I'm not his only son.'

Laura pulled another paper from the sheaf. 'Birth certificate. This is you, isn't it?'

Lucas's skin prickled. Curiosity had pulled Skye closer, and she was at his elbow now, reading what he was. Lucas Harrington Hastings. His date of birth. His place of birth. Father, Ralph Hastings. Mother, Genevieve Hastings.

Lucas shook his head. 'I never met my father. He died before I was born. But he certainly wasn't a duke. I'm sure my mother would have told me that. My mother and I moved around a lot. But I've never heard of…' he pointed to the address that was listed among the papers '… Costley Hall.' He shook his head again. 'I think Mr Cunningham has got me mixed up with someone else.'

Skye sucked in a deep breath next to him and he realised she'd pulled her phone from her pocket.

'What? What is it?'

Her eyes met his. She turned her phone around slowly. 'You might not have met him…' Her words tailed off and as he saw the image on the screen he realised why. The Duke of Mercia—wherever that was—was literally an older version of him.

He blinked then peered a little closer, looking at the distinct green eyes, skin tone and shape of face. He leaned back.

'This is one of those practical jokes, isn't it? Some con for the new guy in the place.' He looked at Skye. 'Did you do this? We haven't met before—is this how you initiate your new staff?' He was starting to feel a bit angry now. He thrust a hand out. 'Have you looked at the board in A&E? There's no time for this, no matter how good a con you think it is. And here?' He pointed to the now empty scanning room. 'This is hardly the place.'

Skye's face pinched.

'Take a breath,' said Laura from the sidelines. 'Mr Hastings, I think you probably need to sit down.'

'I need to sit down?' He spun around. 'I need to sit down?' His voice was rising in pitch. 'Who even are you guys? Some pranksters? This is ridiculous.'

The male policeman put a very firm grip on Lucas's arm. 'Mr Hastings, calm down.'

Lucas threw out his other arm, sending the paperwork scattering on the floor. He was caught in one of those stupid TV prank shows. Or something even worse. He had patients to see. He had notes to write up. Most of all, he had no time for this. And the fact that the new colleague he'd actually considered attractive a few hours ago was in on it made it even more annoying.

'I have work to do,' he declared.

There was an expletive from the floor at his feet. He looked down. Skye was picking up the papers he had scattered. One was clutched in her hand. She stood up, pushing her hair, which had escaped from her tie, back from her face.

'You bet you do,' she said. The tone of her voice stopped him dead.

The look on her face was stuck between incredulous, scornful and laughing. She held the paper up for him. 'Because if this is true... Lucas Hastings?' She said the word with a question in her voice. 'You're the new Duke of Mercia, and a potential billionaire.'

CHAPTER TWO

SKYE WAS ASTOUNDED. But clearly not as much as Lucas, who stood shaking his head. The paper she held was a letter from Mr Cunningham's solicitors' firm, outlining exactly what the will and testament meant for Lucas. It was clear that his intention had been to give this to Lucas. Unfortunately, it looked like that might not happen for a while.

They'd both gone back to A&E to complete their shift. She'd tried to talk to him about it, but Lucas was either in denial or just wasn't ready to believe it.

In the meantime, Skye was looking around at the place she loved and realising that, for the most part, it had lost its shine for her.

Losing her mum had been a pivotal moment for Skye. She was comfortable at The Harlington. She was comfortable in her rented flat. But did she want to spend the rest of her life feeling comfortable?

A few years before, when she'd been looking to make some savings, she'd tried different kinds of nursing—doing bank shifts for a Harley Street clinic, covering post-operative shifts a couple of weekends a month. It had paid well, and they'd offered her a full-time job. But the clients weren't always particularly nice, treating her more like a servant than a nurse, and she'd known it wasn't for her. So, it was time to look again.

She was sitting in the hospital canteen on a break, scrolling through job adverts on her laptop, when she felt a tap on the shoulder. 'Can I join you?'

For a good-looking guy, Lucas looked awful. He had dark circles under his eyes and it was clear he hadn't slept the last few nights.

'Sure,' she said, then shifted a little when he didn't take the chair opposite her like she expected and instead sat down next to her. He was carrying two cups of coffee and two scones.

'I came prepared,' he said and pulled a face. 'I want to say sorry for accusing you of pulling a fast one on me. I honestly thought this was some kind of joke.' He gave a sigh.

'Turns out the joke is what I thought was my normal life.'

If this had been someone she knew better Skye would already have been hugging him right now. But she'd barely met Lucas. It wouldn't be appropriate, no matter how broken he looked.

She accepted the coffee and scone with a nod. 'I've been a nurse too long not to be suspicious of someone who comes bearing scones.'

He nodded. 'You're entirely right. I'm here to see if I can bend your ear for a bit. Or, as my favourite teacher used to say, have a blether.'

She smiled at the phrase. 'Blether away,' she said as she pushed her laptop away, and started buttering the scone.

'Have you told anyone what happened the other day?' The question was tentative.

'Of course not.' She looked at him. 'That was an entirely personal matter. I wouldn't tell anyone about that.'

He didn't even try to hide the audible sigh of relief.

She nudged him with her elbow. 'Eat your scone.'

She'd just got here and had plenty of time

left on her break. Lucas clearly needed someone to talk to, and even though she was just
back at work, and had doubts about a million things, it was kind of flattering that he'd
picked her.

Lucas started eating and took a sip of his
coffee. His shoulders visibly relaxed and she
could tell the tension was starting to leave
his body.

'So,' she started, 'should I call you Duke?'

He groaned. 'Don't. I have no idea what's
going on.'

'How's Mr Cunningham?'

'Still very sick. The surgery to relieve the
pressure on his brain was a success, and he
also had further surgery to replace one of his
hips and set his fractures. But his lung collapsed and he had to have repair work done
on his spleen. Apparently, he's regained consciousness on a few occasions, but they're
pretty much keeping him sedated to let him
heal.'

She studied Lucas's face. Talking about
patients was easy for him, but talking about
himself and his own life…?

'Is there someone else in the company that
can help you?'

He nodded. 'I have an appointment tomorrow. Hopefully, this has all just been a big mistake.'

She took a slow breath. 'People tend not to make mistakes when it comes to money and titles.' She'd finished one half of her scone and spread some jam on the second half. 'So, have you spoken to your mother?'

He cringed. He actually cringed, before leaning his head on his hand and looking at her. 'So, my mum is a bit of a unique individual.'

Skye couldn't help the small smile that appeared on her face at the unusual description. She set down her coffee cup and looked at him. 'And what does that mean?'

He sighed. 'It means that I've left her sixteen voicemails and emailed half a dozen times. I'm not sure if she's in Italy or Spain right now.'

Skye sat back in her chair. 'Wow,' she said simply, her brain whirling. She'd been close to her mother. It was part of the reason that when her mother had been given a terminal diagnosis, Skye had been determined to nurse her herself. She was wise enough to know that families came in all shapes and sizes with differing dynamics, but she couldn't imagine her mother ever disappearing on her like that.

'Are you close?' she asked, almost afraid of the answer.

He waved one hand. 'We moved about a lot. I think I told you that before. My mother was always wanting to jet off somewhere, so this isn't so unusual.'

Skye shifted on her chair a little. 'You moved around a lot?' she reiterated.

He nodded.

'Why do you think that was?' As soon as she'd asked the question, she almost wanted to pull it back. It was too personal—and definitely none of her business. But, then again, Lucas had asked if he could talk to her.

Because she hadn't been here the last few months, she had no idea how Lucas had settled into his new job and new surroundings. Maybe there hadn't been time yet to strike up any friendships. Was it so wrong to be his listening ear?

Over her years in nursing, Skye had learned that there were times when she should just listen, and there were times when she should ask questions. The questions almost always circled back to whoever she was talking to, in a way that gave them a chance to come to their own conclusions.

Lucas had frozen. He didn't answer. Skye immediately felt guilty. Maybe he wasn't ready for this.

She'd tried to imagine being in his shoes. To have someone appear and ask unexpected questions about family. To impart knowledge that things might not be as she'd always imagined. Then, to throw on top, the chance of some kind of title and estate?

Even Skye had to admit that might feel as though her legs had been swept clean out from under her.

Lucas licked his lips. 'I thought she was just restless,' he admitted. 'That she was always looking for the next adventure, the next place.'

'And now?' she asked.

He lifted his head and stared across at the windows. 'Now, I wonder if she was running. If *we* were running.'

Skye's skin prickled. Of course. It was a natural question to ask.

'I take it you didn't know your mum was married?'

Now, he let out a short laugh. 'Married? Are you joking? My mother has the biggest array of rings you've ever seen. But she never wore a wedding ring. Never wore anything on that finger. She told me my dad had died before I was born, but she also told me that she'd never been married to him. I thought Hastings was my mother's maiden name.' He looked thoughtful for a moment. 'To be honest, I always wondered if my dad was married to someone else and had an affair with my mother. But he just didn't feature in our lives. She barely answered any questions about him, and it was just never a thing.' He was shaking his head now, and Skye was aware that a million other questions would now be circulating.

'So, the Duke? Is it likely that he's your father then?'

'Unless it's normal to look at a photograph of someone and wonder if you're looking in a mirror.' His voice had taken on an exasperated tone.

He gestured towards the laptop. 'Thinking of going somewhere else?'

Skye gave a jerk at the sudden change in topic. Her head had been so into Lucas's internal drama that she'd forgotten she'd left the laptop open. She wasn't even quite sure how to answer. She hadn't really had a chance to talk to any of her colleagues yet about how she was feeling.

'Just thinking about the world in general,' she said blandly.

He gave her a look. A look that told her he was just as smart as she was when it came to listening, and asking the right questions.

'Time for a change?'

She bit her lip. 'It might be. I'm not quite sure yet.' She gave a half-smile. 'My brain can't catch up with the rest of me.'

'You've just got back to work. Do you think you might need time to settle again?'

He hadn't said the words out loud, but somehow she knew he'd heard on the grapevine that her mother had died.

'I don't think I want to settle,' she admitted. 'Settling means getting stuck in a rut. Sometimes the rut gets too comfortable. And if you don't take a step outside, you don't know what opportunities you might miss out on. I tried a few other things before, but they're not what I'm looking for either.'

He gave a slow nod, but his green eyes were fixed on her, looking thoughtful. 'All true. But usually when someone is looking for a new job or a career change…' he paused; it was clear he was choosing his words carefully '…they are enthusiastic about it, or excited?'

Skye let out a hollow laugh. 'Meaning I'm not?'

He held up both hands. 'I wouldn't comment on something I shouldn't. I guess I'm just asking the question.'

She waited for a few moments, mulling things over in her mind. 'I guess I am too.'

He nodded at the other tab that was open—the one that had been revealed when she'd tried to click away from the job adverts. 'And what's the excuse for this then?' He was giving her a most amused grin, showing off his perfect teeth.

She looked back at the screen and sat back in her chair. 'That—' she pointed '—is the dream chair, or maybe it's the dream chaise longue.'

He shuddered. 'Okay, now you're scaring me.'

'What?' she asked, half laughing, half teasing. 'You don't like it?'

She looked back at the image of the Chesterfield chaise longue, covered in dark blue velvet patterned with parrots in red, green, yellow and bright blue. 'It's a work of art,' she argued.

'Of a five-year-old,' he mocked, still grinning at her.

She gave a sigh and waved her hand, then put it on her chest. 'You know how sometimes you just spot something so ridiculous, so unexplainable, but you just love it deep down?'

Now he was looking at her as if she had lost her mind, but she kept going.

'And even though you know that—' she pointed at the price tag '—it's something a million miles out of your league, you tell yourself that if you ever win the lottery and money isn't an object any more, that's what you'd spend it on. Just because.' She loved the expression on his face right now, as if he couldn't really understand if she was joking or not. 'Anyway, you know they're called "feature" chairs or "accent" chairs.'

He leaned a little closer, giving her a really good view of just how green his eyes were, and the fact he had eyelashes some girls might kill for. 'So, you're telling me the parrot feature chair is your lottery ticket?'

She gave him her sincerest nod. 'In a heartbeat,' she said without a second of hesitation.

He sat back in his chair, 'Wow,' he murmured, his eyes flicking back to the screen in bewilderment.

Inside, she was still smiling. There was something nice about such tiny moments of connection, even if they were in jest. As she shifted in her seat and he lowered his hands, her fingers brushed against his. It made her catch her breath, and she glanced at her watch, knowing it was time for her to leave.

'Can I say one thing?'

'Of course,' he said.

'When you get hold of your mum—' her voice trembled a little '—no matter what she says, don't be angry. That time is gone, but you've still got her. Just love her.'

She'd overstepped. She knew she'd overstepped, but she couldn't help how her current position made her feel. She'd give anything for one more hug, one more conversation, even though her mum had died in a comfortable, respectful way, and entirely the way she'd wanted.

He gave a slow nod. She couldn't even guess what the myriad of emotions were that flickered behind his eyes. 'Can you come?' he asked.

She picked up her laptop. 'Where?'

'Tomorrow. To the lawyers. Can you come with me?'

He looked so vulnerable. So torn about everything. Skye was off-duty tomorrow, and she wondered if he already knew that, and this had been why he'd sought her out today.

'Of course,' she replied, writing her number down on a scrap of paper from her pocket. 'Just let me know when, and where.'

As she made to walk away, he pointed at her laptop. 'And don't worry,' he added. 'Your secret is safe with me.'

And as she hugged her laptop close to her chest and headed back to A&E, she somehow knew it was.

He was pacing. Lucas knew he was pacing. He glanced at his watch again and breathed a sigh of relief as he glimpsed a bright red wool coat as Skye emerged from the underground. She pulled her bobble hat from her head and gave him a grin as she tried to fix her hair. The temperature had plummeted in London in the last couple of days and the first few flakes of snow were falling.

'Brr...' Skye shuddered. 'How's Mr Cunningham?'

Lucas gave a nod. 'Improving, but very slowly. They're weaning him off the sedation. He's got a chest infection now too, on top of everything else, but his levels of consciousness are improving.'

Skye gave a nod, her blonde hair already covered in tiny flakes of snow. 'That sounds a bit better. But still in no shape to talk to you?'

He shook his head. 'I wouldn't even go there.' He glanced up at the blue glass building in front of them. 'The lawyers were keen for me to wait until he can deal with things. But I think they're being unrealistic about his recovery time.' He shrugged his shoulders. 'I'm not Mr Cunningham's doctor, so it's not for me to have that conversation with them. I just told them someone else would need to bring me up to speed.'

It struck him that he'd only ever seen Skye in work clothes. Her fitted red coat, black boots and blonde hair were more than enough to turn a few heads in the street. He felt strangely protective of her.

'Thank you for doing this for me,' he said quickly.

'No problem,' she said. 'I've gone through some of this myself already. It's not nice, I can't lie. But hopefully it will help, having someone with you.'

She gave him a curious look. 'Did you get hold of your mum?'

He gave an exasperated sigh. 'Yes, and no. She's apparently in a place with no phone signal. An exclusive yoga resort. But she replied to one of my many emails—' he held up a finger '—with the birth certificate attached, and said that yes, the Duke was my father, but they'd had a falling-out years ago and she didn't want anything to do with him.'

Skye's brow wrinkled. 'There has to be more to it than that.'

'Oh, there is. But she's not telling me any more at the moment. Says it's all in the past, and she'll be back in London soon and we can catch up then.'

Skye stood still for the longest time. He had no idea what was going on in her head, but he saw her give a visible swallow and then a nod. She looked up at the building. 'Shall we go ahead?'

'Let's go.' He held the door open for her, and pushed the buttons when they moved into the lift to climb to the fifth floor.

When the doors opened again it was to a sleek reception desk, where two members of staff in dark suits and with immaculate hair and make-up were waiting for them.

One stood up. 'Your Grace.' She gave a nod

and Lucas felt as if he'd stepped into an alternative universe. He glanced over his shoulder. Nope. No one else here. She'd definitely been talking to him.

A bewildered grin appeared on Skye's face as she started walking after the receptionist. 'Come on,' she prompted in a low voice, keeping the smile in place.

His feet had welded themselves to the polished floor. His mouth was dry. For a few seconds he wondered if he could walk out again. But Skye's red coat was leading the way into another room.

He hurried to catch up, moving into a room with two stern-faced men, a woman with a notepad and a large table that was clearly meant to be intimidating. There were only six chairs in the room, and this table was far too large to only seat six.

Lucas sat in the chair that he was gestured to, and accepted the offer of coffee. Skye slid off her red coat. She'd dressed for the occasion, and he suspected she was better prepared for this than he was. She was wearing tailored black trousers and a cream satin blouse. One of the men half glared across the table at them both.

'Roger Phillips,' he said stiffly. 'And this is my colleague, William Bruce.'

There was an air of disapproval in his tone that Lucas didn't like. Was this the man he'd spoken to on the phone, who'd originally refused to meet him? Lucas wasn't normally short with people, but by the time he'd phoned the lawyers' office to request a meeting he'd been stressed and confused. When he'd been brushed off, he'd mentioned that he was surprised that a London solicitors' had no resilience built in, and surely one man wasn't the only person familiar with each individual case. An appointment had been found, even though it was apparently resented.

'Lucas Hastings,' he replied, 'And this is my colleague, Skye Carter.'

Mr Phillips's brow furrowed so badly Lucas was sure he could plant seeds in it. 'You do realise that everything that is discussed in here today is confidential?' He was actually glaring at Skye, who seemed completely nonplussed.

This woman had worked in one of London's busiest A&Es for seven years. He doubted very much that a grumpy man would have any impact.

He kept his voice level as a steaming cup of coffee was put in front of them, the coffee grounds fragrant in the air. 'I'm a doctor, my colleague is a nurse. Please don't lecture us on confidentiality.'

Mr Bruce gave a short laugh, making both Lucas and Skye turn their heads in his direction. He smiled. 'This might be fun.'

Lucas shifted in his chair, his mind going back to the day he'd been first told about all this and thinking it was some kind of joke. The laughing lawyer felt like a continuation of the joke.

'Honestly,' he muttered, 'it's like being in an alternate reality.'

Skye side-eyed him. 'Better be chocolate in this reality or I'm calling quits,' she said under her breath.

Mr Phillips's face was turning redder by the second.

'Can someone please get to the point?' Lucas sighed.

Mr Phillips started talking in a pompous voice. 'Mr Hastings, we're meeting you today because ten months ago the Duke of Mercia, Ralph Ignatius Cornwell Hastings, died. Our company is the executor of the Duke's will.'

Lucas didn't speak. He didn't have anything to add. He already knew the bones of the story.

'The Duke did not have any other children. Therefore, the majority of his estate has been willed to you, his son, Lucas Harrington Hastings.' His gaze narrowed. 'We will, of course, require a DNA sample to ensure we have the right individual.'

Lucas raised his eyebrows. 'The right person, with the right name, date of birth and birth certificate, which is mine?'

'It's a legal matter,' snapped Mr Phillips.

Mr Bruce leaned over the table. 'Do you have an accountant?'

'What?' Lucas shook his head. This was like an episode of a comedy series. 'I'm a doctor. Of course I don't have an accountant.'

'I can recommend one,' said Mr Bruce with a wave of his hand.

Skye closed her hand over his, clearly trying to centre him back to the madness in the room. 'Can you tell Lucas what is involved in the estate, as you call it?'

A bound collection of papers was passed over to Lucas. He opened it. The first asset listed was Costley Hall, along with its value, running costs and staff. He gulped, trying not to seem overwhelmed.

He turned over the page. Details of a number of vineyards, wineries and associated companies. More pages—more properties. More pages—lands and gardens. More pages—company names, all based in locations he hadn't even heard of.

He looked up and lifted the bound papers. 'So, what does this actually mean for me?'

'There's the issue of inheritance tax,' said Mr Bruce, scribbling a note on a piece of paper and passing it to Lucas. The sum made his eyes water. If he worked as a doctor his entire lifetime he wouldn't be able to earn the sum he was supposed to pay in inheritance tax.

'Is there a timescale to settling the estate?' asked Skye. She was sitting a little straighter now and had a serious look on her face— she'd clearly seen the figure on that piece of paper too.

'Once the DNA sample is confirmed, the monies and legal documents will be handed over to Mr Hastings's team,' said Mr Phillips.

'And if he doesn't have a team?' probed Skye.

Mr Phillips looked up from hooded lids. 'Then he'd better get one.'

Silence in the office while Lucas digested that last statement. He really didn't like this guy.

'So, Mr Cunningham normally deals with all this?'

Mr Bruce nodded. 'Albert Cunningham has been the Duke's solicitor for more than fifty years. He knows everything about the estate and companies.'

'And the title?' Skye's question came out of nowhere and all eyes turned towards her.

Mr Phillips cleared his throat. 'The title passes to the oldest son, which means that, as of ten months ago, Lucas Harrington Hastings has been the Duke of Mercia.'

'Is there a reason you took so long to let him know?' Skye was practically perched on the edge of her chair now.

Mr Phillips waved his hand. 'An estate of this size takes considerable work. Things can't be done overnight.'

But it seemed that Skye had no intention of letting this go.

'I have some experience in these matters,' she said coldly. 'Shouldn't the next of kin be informed of a death in the family as soon as possible?' As the lawyers exchanged glances she kept going. 'Ten months hardly seems right.' She pulled a piece of paper from her pocket and unfolded it. 'In fact, Mr Cunningham had this letter on his person at the time of the attack. It's dated—' she looked at it theatrically before straightening '—eight months ago, informing Lucas of the death of the Duke, the approximate value of the estate and the fact he'd inherited the title.'

Mr Phillips's face was still red. 'Our colleague was presumptuous. Details had to be checked.'

'Eight months is a long time to check details,' Skye observed.

Silence fell again.

'Who has looked after the estate, properties and companies for the last ten months?' asked Lucas.

Mr Bruce gave a half-smile. 'Everyone employed by the Duke's companies has continued in their role. The companies have continued to trade as normal.' He cleared his throat. 'There are a few other factors to consider.'

'Such as?' Lucas's skin prickled. Somehow, he knew this wasn't going to be good.

'The Duke's will also grants properties to some of those who were in his employment. A housekeeper and groundsman at Costley

Hall have inherited a cottage on the grounds. As has the head groom.' He pressed his lips together for a second. 'There is also a spousal maintenance payment.' He looked up, his dark eyes meeting Lucas's.

It took a few seconds for the penny to drop. 'To my mother?'

He'd always wondered how she'd managed to maintain her lifestyle. He'd asked on numerous occasions, because he'd never actually known his mother to work, but she'd waved her hand and spoken about 'family money', saying it in such a way as to imply it had come from her deceased parents.

Now, it seemed it had been coming from the ex-husband and father of Lucas—the man she'd let him think was dead.

'I should mention,' said Mr Bruce quickly, 'that one of the stipulations in the will is that you continue with the payment to your mother.'

Lucas let out a sound he couldn't even decipher himself. Continue to support the mother who'd lied to him and, even now, couldn't bring herself to come home and tell the truth.

'The Duke,' he said suddenly, 'how did he die?'

He was a doctor and it had just occurred to

him that, all of a sudden, he was about to find out about half of his family genetics. He'd always wondered. Toyed with those family DNA tests which could also test for genetic conditions. Lots of things could be inherited. So, this thought had occurred to him like a giant wrecking ball hitting his head side on.

Mr Bruce took a theatrical pause. Lucas—who was used to being calm and collected—was visualising dragging the man across his imposing table.

'The Duke had an abdominal aortic aneurysm. He collapsed at home and died before he reached hospital.'

'Had he been screened?' asked Lucas without hesitation. Abdominal aortic aneurysm screening had been available in England for a number of years for all men over sixty-five.

Mr Bruce gave an uncomfortable shiver. 'That information is not available.'

No. *Unfortunately...* No, *I'm sorry to say.* Mr Bruce didn't even have the curtesy to try and soften his words.

Lucas stood up abruptly. He'd heard enough for today.

Mr Phillips looked startled. 'We've still to make arrangements for the DNA test.'

Skye stood up too. 'And we will. Although—'

she glanced over at Lucas and back to the law-yers '—if you knew the Duke personally, I'm sure you can both see the family resemblance.'

Lucas knew there was a hint of a smile on his face. He'd brought Skye along for moral support, and she'd done that in spades. She was totally unaffected by the attitude in the room, or the amount of money that had been shown on the paperwork they'd both looked at.

She shot the lawyers her brightest smile as she tucked her arm into Lucas's. 'Gentle-men, if you'll excuse us, we have another appointment.'

Mr Phillips was clearly annoyed. It was strange, as he hadn't wanted to meet Lucas in the first place and didn't seem particularly adept at answering any of the questions that had been put to him. It struck Lucas that this company had likely always made a large part of their income from the Duke. Might they have deliberately delayed things to allow that to continue? It wasn't such a ridiculous thought. He couldn't wait to get out of here.

As they headed for the lifts, Mr Phillips followed them, still talking in an indignant voice. The two receptionists at the main desk stood as they walked past and Lucas had a flash of memory.

'Mr Hastings, we have not finished. You still have to be verified...'

Lucas spun around. 'We've already made it clear that we are finished for today.' He kept his voice low and steady. 'I'll be in touch about the DNA test, once I've had some independent advice.'

Mr Phillips made a derisive sound and Lucas knew he'd touched a nerve. Of course he would take some other advice—that was entirely his right, and the only sound thing to do. Mr Phillips gave him a look that could only be described as a sneer, and opened his mouth to speak again. But Lucas cut him dead.

'And in future, Mr Phillips, I would appreciate if you could address me by my proper title, which I believe is—' he raised his eyebrows '—Your Grace.'

And with that he stepped inside the lift alongside Skye and kept his eyes looking straight ahead as the doors slid closed.

CHAPTER THREE

SKYE READ THROUGH the application form for the fifth time and finally pressed send. It was the fourth one she'd completed, and she wasn't entirely sure that any of them would prove to be the right move for her. This one was for a job as a practice nurse in a GP surgery. She'd also applied for district nurse training, to be a nurse lecturer for student nurses, and for a training post as an endoscopy nurse. The whole world was out there, but she just didn't know the path to take.

Part of her wondered if it was running away. Getting away from The Harlington might help clear her thoughts. Because of what had happened with her mum dying, it was almost as if she associated her workplace with all those memories. It was a strange connection, and one other people might not get, but it was definitely in her head.

So, no matter what job came up, a fresh start might just be the change that she needed.

'What's that sigh for?' asked Lucas as he pushed a box of doughnuts under her nose. It was huge. A staff A&E delight, with twenty-four to choose from. She plucked a raspberry one from the box and looked over his shoulder to see if anyone else was around. Thankfully, the staffroom was empty.

'Just finished another application form,' she said.

'You're serious about this?'

She nodded. 'If I were Dorothy, I'd be looking for the Emerald City right now, but not sure of the direction.' She gestured to the computer. 'I've just got to hope that fate will have a hand in where I end up.'

She took a bite of her doughnut and looked at Lucas again. She'd heard a few colleagues talking about him the other day, wondering if he was dating anyone, and she hadn't liked the way it had made her stomach clench. She still found him as good-looking as the first day she'd met him, and when she heard his Scottish accent down the corridor it made the tiny hairs on her arms stand up to attention. The dark circles had disappeared from under his eyes now, and he seemed more chilled.

'Any word from your favourite solicitors?' It had been two weeks since they'd been at the office.

He nodded. 'I got a letter yesterday. The DNA test told them what they needed to know.' He groaned. 'It's also confirmed to me that I now have a one in three chance of developing the same condition as my now confirmed father.'

Skye leaned over and squeezed his hand. 'The danger of knowing too much about family genetics is overthinking it. There's too much that's new right now. Take some time to consider things.'

She was trying to be logical for him, hoping that if the shoe were on the other foot this was the kind of thing he would say to her.

'So, what happens now?'

He sighed. 'Now, I get to go and see Costley Hall. Want to come with me on Saturday?'

They'd fallen into an easy friendship, working alongside each other but still keeping each other's secrets for the past few weeks. Skye was aware that colleagues were likely talking about their secret whispering, but she didn't really care.

Was it too personal to agree and see where the previous Duke had lived?

He nudged her. 'You know you want to.'

She rolled her eyes. 'I do, actually. I was just wondering if I should try and show more decorum.'

'Decorum?' He laughed. 'Have you met me? I'm the guy with the broad Scottish accent. As soon as I set foot on the estate, they'll likely all run screaming from the building. I know nothing about the aristocracy. I have no idea what they actually expect of me—if anything.'

Skye gave him a curious look. 'Why on earth would you feel like that? You're a good guy. A doctor. True, you might not have known your father was a Duke and that it was a title you would inherit but, let's face it, the fault there lies with the adults in your life, not with you.'

He raised one eyebrow and smiled. 'Oh, call it like you see it. Don't hold back.'

Skye swallowed a bite of her doughnut. 'Have you managed to pin your mother down yet?'

They'd talked about this on a few occasions and it was clear to them both that Lucas's mother was using avoidance tactics right now. Skye was beginning to feel annoyed by this woman she'd never met. This was hard enough for Lucas. His mother could at least be truthful and let him know the entire story.

He shook his head and grinned at her. 'I get the distinct impression that if she ever appears you might bodily pin her to the ground yourself.'

Skye nodded. 'It's crossed my mind.' She pinned a smile on her face. 'But let's forget about that. I'd be happy to come along and see Costley Hall on Saturday. Let's just hope we can actually get in.' She tilted her head. 'Have you seen Mr Cunningham?'

Lucas sighed. 'I have—he's much improved, and devastated that he's lost his Aston Martin. It was one of only a few made.'

'You managed to talk about the Aston Martin instead of your father?'

Lucas pulled a face. 'It's hard. I'm not officially his doctor, but I did treat him. I don't think it's right for me to ask him questions when he's still in the hospital. Especially when I think there's something off about his colleagues.'

Skye stood up and brushed some sugar from her uniform. 'Oh, you've got that right. That was one of the strangest meetings I've attended in my life.' She let out a wry laugh. 'And I've been to our Trust's leadership groups.'

He rolled his eyes. 'The ones where they make you all hum, or the ones where they tell you to picture yourself as an animal?'

'Both,' she said, laughing.

'What were you?' he asked.

Skye could feel heat rising in her cheeks. 'Oh, don't.'

'Go on,' he teased. 'Tell me what animal you picked.'

She waved her hand. 'It was a bad day for me. I was running late after a flat tyre on my car, was covered in muck from changing my tyre at the side of the road and had missed out on the coffee. Honestly, when she picked on me and asked me to choose an animal, my mind went entirely blank. You know how that sometimes happens when you go to put your pin number in a card terminal in a shop? Nothing there at all?'

He nodded and she pointed to her chest. 'Well, that was me. Skye Carter. Human being that's been on the planet for thirty entire years, has passed exams, got a degree, rents a house, manages bills and a budget and—' she flicked her fingers in the air '—nothing. A big fat nothing.'

'So, what did you say?'

She laughed. 'Oh, the guy sitting next to me—who I'd never set eyes on before, and have never set eyes on again—did me the favour of mumbling "beaver" under his breath. So that was me. Before my brain started functioning again. I became a beaver.'

Lucas started to laugh.

'Not one of my finest moments.'

His shoulders were twitching up and down. 'Seriously?' He reached a hand up to wipe a tear from his eye.

Skye was still laughing too. 'Seriously. The A&E sister, who is sitting on a Trust leadership course with all these other senior NHS managers, told her colleagues her most associated animal was a beaver.'

She walked over to the sink and washed her hands, glancing over her shoulder at him. 'I try not to talk about it, but I'm pretty sure the rest of those people still tell friends and colleagues that story.'

There was something so nice about this. Just…chatting. Having someone she felt comfortable around. It was hard to ignore how wide his grin was, or the colour of those eyes. But she was doing her best to focus on being a friend for Lucas. He'd had a shock. His main family relationship had changed for ever because of this news. And he was still on a learning curve about what all this meant.

He'd only been in London for a few months, and she'd been on leave for a good part of that, but she got the impression he hadn't yet made any good friends around here. It could be tricky for medical staff, particularly when their training programmes could mean moving every year and working across different cities. Lucas was proving easy to be around.

After the trauma of losing her mum, and the secondary part of working through all the practical issues, having a different focus was good for her. Nursing a parent, and being the only one to deal with everything afterwards, had been draining in a way it was hard to explain. Even before she'd returned to work, some days had seemed as if there was nothing else to focus on.

Now, while she still had a few things to sort out, she could let her thoughts drift into Lucas's crazy situation. She could get angry for him. She could help him plan. And this meant she wasn't constantly thinking about fighting with the gas supplier to get a final bill when they kept telling her they would only speak to the account holder—even though the account holder, her mother, was dead.

Skye gave a small smile. 'Why don't you let me go and talk to Mr Cunningham so you don't feel as if there is a conflict of interest? If I think he's still too unwell I won't ask a thing. But if he's doing better, I could find out some general information for you.'

'Aren't lawyers like doctors—client privilege?'

She pressed her lips together. 'Probably. But your dad was the client, not you. I can ask him some general questions about the Duke and let him know we're going to see the house.' She nodded. 'Let me see what I can do.'

'Oh, no,' said Lucas, folding his arms with a grin. 'You've got that look again.'

'What look?' Skye tried to appear innocent.

'You know exactly what look,' he joked. 'The one that means you're plotting. No one is safe.'

She smiled again as she headed for the door. 'And that's exactly what I want everyone to think.' She winked. 'Keeps them all on their toes.'

* * *

Lucas was feeling strangely nervous. Not the kind of flutters that occasionally came with the first day on a new job. Nope. This was a deep down, heavy sensation in the pit of his stomach.

He was glad he wasn't doing this alone. Skye had jumped into the car with two steaming cups of coffee and some banana loaf that she'd had a go at making herself. 'My mum's recipe,' she said as she handed some over, wrapped in tinfoil. 'To be honest, I'm crap at making it, but I keep trying. It's a bit wonky. I've also got a recipe for yoghurt loaf. And one for lentil soup. But don't you always feel that when you make it yourself, it never tastes as good as when someone else makes it?'

She was talking nineteen-to-the-dozen. Was Skye nervous? Today her hair was skimming her shoulders in soft waves and her lips matched her red coat. A waft of orange and spice drifted in his direction. The perfume suited her. And he couldn't help but smile.

He looked down at the squinty slice of banana loaf on his lap. 'Thanks. I'm sure it will be great.' He broke a piece off and ate it as he pulled back into the traffic.

The journey to Costley Hall took over

ninety minutes. It was just on the outskirts of London, where the mass of buildings started to turn into the green of the countryside.

'I got some gossip,' Skye said as she watched the countryside slip past.

'What?'

'From Mr Cunningham.'

'No way—did you con information out of him?'

Skye grinned. 'I didn't con any information out of him. I asked him about an old friend. I also gave him a warning about his business colleagues, but I suspect he's wise to them. It's maybe why he hasn't retired. He might have referred to them as whippersnappers.'

Lucas laughed out loud. 'What?'

She beamed. 'Whippersnappers. It's a great word. Exactly the kind of word a very well brought up man in his eighties might use.' She leaned back against the leather seats in the car and sighed. 'I think Mr Cunningham might have been a bit of a catch in his day.'

Lucas gave her a surprised look, but she'd turned to face him as she continued. 'Can you imagine him, driving about in his super spy Aston Martin? I bet he was popular.'

Lucas took a sip of his coffee. 'So, the gossip. What did you find out?'

'Oh, yes.' She looked perfectly pleased with herself. 'The Duke of Mercia. Do you know why he's called that?'

'Er, no,' replied Lucas, not taking his eyes off the road.

'Well, Mercia is like Wessex—you know that name that was given to Edward—Earl of Wessex? It's an old England name. In Anglo-Saxon times, from back around the eight hundreds.'

Lucas frowned. 'So where was Mercia? And where was Wessex? I thought dukes were supposed to be named after real places, like Edinburgh or Cornwall.'

She shrugged. 'Wessex—depending on what map you look at, and what point in time—covered, at one point, London, Winchester, most of the south part of England, although I think there was some fighting between the various parts. Mercia, on the other hand—' she nodded and gave a knowing smile '—was bigger. It covered Chester, Lincoln, Worcester—basically a large part of the middle of the country.'

'So, my father was named a duke of some ancient Anglo-Saxon kingdom.' He wrinkled his nose. 'I have told you that I keep thinking this is all just an elaborate joke, haven't I?'

She nodded. 'On multiple occasions. Still not a joke.'

He gave her a sideways glance. 'What else did you find out?'

Skye pulled a face. 'It was a bit of a two-way exchange.'

He raised his eyebrows. 'Sold me out, did you?'

'In a heartbeat.' She smiled, her blue eyes connecting with his. He caught his breath. It was the look on her face. Yes, they were joking. This was how they'd quickly learned to be around each other. But, deep down, and even though he'd only known her a few weeks, he had a good feeling about Skye Carter. She didn't strike him as a girl who would sell anyone out.

'He was a good friend of your father,' she started, then took a breath. 'And I got the general impression that they liked and respected each other.'

There was something in her tone. 'But?' He glanced at her, but her expression was fixed. 'Skye?' They rounded a long curve in the country road. 'What are you not saying?'

She licked her lips and let out a long, slow breath. 'I could be very wrong, but I got a feeling it could have been more—not that Mr Cunningham said that.'

Pieces of the jigsaw puzzle that Lucas hadn't even begun to fit together assembled in his head.

'Oh?' he said as they slotted together. Then, 'Ooh…'

Silence followed in the car and Lucas's nose wrinkled. 'I wonder if that's why my mother isn't saying much.'

Skye looked at him. 'It could be, and I might be entirely wrong. It was just a feeling I got…a sense.'

As they neared the area where Costley Hall was situated Lucas spoke again. 'Did you find out anything else from Mr Cunningham?'

'Just very general things. Costley Hall was always going to be yours. The intention was always that you would inherit the title. They had no idea that your mother had told you that your father was dead. The Duke tried to make contact on frequent occasions, to try and stay in touch, but everything was always on your mother's terms. When you turned eighteen, he tried to find you again, but your mother wouldn't let him know where you were, or what you were doing.'

Lucas had the oddest sensation. As if someone was reaching into his chest and twisting his heart. His father had never been a focus in his life. He'd been told his father was dead, and that had been the end of it. Even when he'd asked questions growing up, his mother had made it clear the conversation was finished. He'd accepted it. There had been no point in pursuing things. He'd had no reason to think there was.

'There!' Skye pointed at a road sign for Costley Hall and Lucas indicated to turn in. They passed through a wide set of iron gates and followed an avenue with trees on either side. It went on for ever.

'Is this place hidden?' asked Skye.

'I have no idea,' said Lucas, finally slowing as a building on the right-hand side of the road emerged. It was a stone cottage, well maintained, painted white, with a bright red door. It was relatively large for a cottage and had clearly been extended over the years.

'Do you think that's where the groundsman and housekeeper live?' Skye asked. 'It looks lovely.'

The car had almost drawn to a halt, and Lucas realised that he and Skye were practically staring into someone's home. He gave himself a shake and continued down the road.

After another few minutes the trees fell away and the grey road changed to a dusky white colour. As they followed the curve of the driveway, they got the full impact of Costley Hall.

It was like a house from a film or TV series. A grand building with three floors and glistening windows. Circular steps were at the front, pillars over the entranceway and wooden doors that looked too big to be practical. Skye let out a breath, and her head nodded up and down as she counted.

'Okay, there's ten sets of windows on either side of the doors—just how big is this place?'

'Don't ask me,' said Lucas as he swallowed uncomfortably. A sign for the stables and gardens indicated another road which branched off around the side of the hall towards the back. The front gardens were pristinely manicured.

'Someone is clearly an expert in topiary around here,' murmured Skye as she pointed to the array of round, spiral and pyramid-shaped bushes and shrubs on display. What was even more attractive was the fact that most of them were tipped with the lightest dusting of snow. She held her hands out. 'Is it time for snow already?'

Lucas smiled. 'Sure is—next you'll be getting your advent calendar out.'

They climbed out of the car and just stood for a moment, both staring up at the hall, which seemed to have blindsided both of them.

Lucas's voice was a little nervous. 'Should we look around?'

They both started walking. Lucas looked back at where he'd parked his car. It looked abandoned near the fountain at the front of the house. The circular road around it was clearly designed to allow cars to turn, but he hadn't been exactly sure where to park. It wasn't obvious.

Skye stopped walking and held up a hand in a stop sign. 'Picture calendar or chocolate calendar?'

It took him just a second to realise she was referring to his previous comment. He was glad. It seemed she was trying to distract him from the hugeness of all this.

'Honestly, I prefer the wine one a friend bought me one year.'

'You had a wine advent calendar?'

He nodded. 'It was delivered to a place I was renting, and was actually addressed to my mother. But she was spending her winter in the Maldives, so I shared it with my roommate.'

As he said the words, something passed across her eyes.

'My male roommate,' he added quickly, then wondered why he'd felt obliged to qualify it.

They were friends. New friends. But would there be a chance of something else? The more time he spent around Skye Carter, the more time he wanted to spend around her. She was smart, fun, and not slow to let anyone know what she thought. She was also a great nurse, with clinical skills he could rely on.

Maybe it was the point they were both at in their lives that was drawing him to her. He knew she'd just returned to work and was contemplating a change. He'd just had a change thrust upon him that he certainly wasn't prepared for.

Having someone by his side was comforting. And the fact it was Skye? Just made it all the better.

Skye gave a shiver and wrapped her red coat around her a little tighter. 'Should we go inside?'

'Sure,' he said, his stomach clenched as

they walked up the steps to the enormous country house he now officially owned.

He paused, wondering whether to just push the door open or to ring the bell. He didn't want to get off on the wrong foot with anyone, so he used the large door knocker.

'There's technology,' Skye whispered, pointing to a doorbell that clearly had a camera attached.

'Let's see if the door knocker works,' he replied with a shrug.

A few seconds later the huge door was pulled open by a woman with bright blonde hair and a nervous smile. 'Your Grace?' she questioned.

Lucas blinked. For all his bravado at the lawyers' office, he was sure this was an address he wouldn't get used to. He nodded and held out his hand. 'Lucas Hastings,' he said. 'And please call me Lucas.'

The woman licked her pink lips, gave a small nod and shook his hand. He wondered why she was so nervous, and again thought about the father he'd never known. Had his father been a bad boss? Made the staff uncomfortable?

'And this is my friend, Skye Carter,' he added quickly as they stepped inside the door.

The woman shook Skye's hand too. 'I'm Olivia Bell, the housekeeper of Costley Hall, and my husband Donald is the groundsman. He'll want to meet you both.' She gave a nervous laugh, and Skye shot Lucas a glance. It was clear they both realised this woman was on edge.

Lucas couldn't help but look upwards. The main entranceway was beyond grand. It reached all the way to the top of the building, where there was a magnificent glass dome. Small yellow, blue and peach-coloured squares of glass decorated the dome, and the sun streaming through made it look as if confetti was dancing on the pale floor.

The walls on the ground floor were wood-panelled, and two magnificent staircases curved up on either side of the entranceway to the first floor. On either side of the entranceway, two gleaming chandeliers lit the way to either side of the house, adding to the otherworldly beauty of the whole place.

It took a moment to take everything in. Lucas glanced at Skye, in part to try and steady his nerves and maintain some normality, but Skye seemed as amazed as he was. She'd already opened her red coat and pushed her blonde hair back from her face. Her eyes were wide and her mouth slightly open.

He took another breath. She was stunning. And it was the first time he'd really noticed. If he'd glanced at her from across the room, he was sure his feet would have been making their way over right now.

'Would you like some tea?' asked Olivia.

'We'd love some tea,' said Skye quickly and the sudden words made Lucas blink away his previous thoughts and focus on what lay ahead.

Olivia nodded. 'I'll show you to the drawing room,' she said, her voice getting slightly higher pitched.

'Actually,' said Lucas, his hand touching her arm gently. 'While we'd love to see round the place, why don't we just follow you to the kitchen and have tea there?'

She seemed a bit worried and Lucas was conscious of trying to put her at ease. He wasn't there to fire them or intimidate them in any way. In an ideal world, he'd like this woman and her husband to be his friends. This was all brand-new, and he wanted to think he could trust the people who were already living in his inherited home.

The housekeeper seemed startled at first,

but then led them through the wide corridors, laid with tiny black and white tiles, to the enormous kitchen. At the heart of the kitchen was a twelve-seated wooden table. The surface of the table was polished, but it held a lifetime's worth of scrapes and dents.

As Olivia hurried around the kitchen Lucas had a look around. The windows looked out over what seemed to be a well-maintained vegetable garden, some greenhouses, and then on to manicured back lawns, with stables off to the side. He sat down at the table with Skye and ran his hand over the surface of the table, wondering if, in another lifetime, he might have made some of these marks and dents.

Skye seemed to read his mind and gently put her hand over his. 'It's a lot,' she said, her smile warm. 'I might need to lie down after seeing all of this place. It feels like what I imagine Cinderella's palace might be like.'

There was the sound of a door opening, and a man appeared, still wearing work clothes. He removed his boots and came over, holding out his hand. 'Your Grace.'

'Lucas,' said Lucas quickly. 'Are you Donald? It's a pleasure to meet you.'

As introductions were made, and Olivia

brought over tea and cakes, she and her husband seemed to hover by the table. Skye gave Lucas a nudge, and he realised what was wrong.

'I'd be delighted if you'd both sit down and join us,' he said quickly. 'I want to hear all about Costley Hall and what you both do here.'

There was a nervous exchange of glances before they both finally sat down. Tea was poured into elegant china cups and saucers, and cake was passed around.

'Tell me about this place,' said Lucas. 'I only know the briefest of details about it, and about my father.'

Donald looked puzzled. 'Albert hasn't told you?'

Lucas cast a quick glance at Skye. They clearly didn't know.

'Albert was injured on his way to the hospital to find me. He's been a patient for a couple of weeks now, and I've had to deal with some of the other lawyers from the practice.'

'You work at the hospital?'

Lucas met their gaze. 'Yes, I'm working at The Harlington. I'm an A&E doctor there, and Skye is one of the charge nurses.'

He could tell from the glances they exchanged that they secretly approved, and he felt an odd sense of relief. He wanted these people to like him.

'Will Albert be okay?' asked Olivia.

Skye smiled. 'He's making a good recovery, but it might be another few weeks. We—' then she looked sideways '—I mean Lucas, hasn't wanted to ask Albert too many questions when he should be focusing on his recovery.'

Donald took a slow breath. 'Well, those lawyers won't have been able to tell you much. The Duke threw them out of here on more than one occasion.'

Lucas looked up sharply and couldn't hide his broad smile. 'I've dealt with them on a few occasions,' he admitted. 'And they haven't become any more palatable.'

This time it was Donald's turn to laugh. 'You're more like your father than anyone expected.'

Lucas's skin prickled. 'I never knew my father,' he said slowly. 'In fact, my mother told me my father was dead. She never said anything about him being a Duke, or that he was even alive.'

Olivia's face pinched. 'Ginny had plans of her own. I've never understood why she didn't let you stay here and grow up in such a wonderful place.'

Lucas tried to remain steady. The fact that Olivia had just referred to his mother as Ginny meant that she'd known her well. He'd only ever heard a few people call her that, and they'd both been old acquaintances. For as long as he could remember, she would introduce herself to people as Genevieve.

He decided not to go down that path. 'What can you tell me about Costley Hall? Obviously, I've never been here before.'

There was another exchange of glances.

'But you were,' said Donald in a soft tone. 'You were here as a baby. But, just before your second birthday, your mother packed her bags and left. The Duke was distraught. Had private investigators searching for you both. Eventually, divorce papers arrived and Albert acted as the Duke's solicitor.'

Olivia gave a small sigh. 'We were surprised. We thought Albert would manage to get you back. To arrange visitation rights for your father. But it just never seemed to happen.'

The air around them was practically flickering. Lucas could sense it, and he knew Skye could too because her hand moved under the table and touched his thigh. Her intention was clearly to keep him calm, but the gesture had the opposite effect. In truth, it took his mind off the conversation they'd just been having and to a completely different place, but this wasn't the time or the place.

He moved his hand over hers and squeezed it.

His thoughts had lingered a few times on Skye applying for other jobs. He didn't like the thought of that. They were a good team at work, and she was the only person who knew about this, and the only person he'd connected with. He didn't want her to leave.

But Lucas knew it wasn't his place to even think about that. He caught a frequent sadness in her eyes at work, and he wondered if it was more about her mother than anything else. Her hand, warm in his, brought him back to the present, and all the things he didn't know about his own life.

'Tell me about the Hall,' he said.

'The history, or the layout?' asked Donald.

'Both,' he replied.

Donald nodded. 'Costley Hall was originally built in the nineteenth century and has changed a number of times over the years. The foundations for this building were laid in 1842 and the internal layout has altered a few times over the years. You'll like this,' he said with the hint of a smile. 'It was used as a hospital in the First World War for wounded soldiers and was run by the then Duchess. In the Second World War it was used as a home for children who were evacuated from London. There are over one hundred rooms, staterooms, bedrooms, two libraries, studies, multiple dining and drawing rooms, as well as a ballroom.'

'Wow, that'll be some heating bill,' said Skye, and as all heads turned towards her, her hand went up to her mouth. 'Oops—' she pulled a face '—did I say that out loud?'

Donald started to laugh. 'You're not joking.' He gave a shrug. 'Just don't ask how many boilers a place like this needs.'

Lucas could feel his skin start to prickle. His hand went up to rub the back of his neck. 'Is there any more help around here?'

Olivia stood up and opened one of the drawers in the dresser, bringing out a large black hardback notebook. She set it down on the table and pushed it towards Lucas.

'We thought you might want some kind of summary. This is a note of everyone employed on the Duke's estate…' She halted suddenly and paused. It was clear she'd forgotten for a moment that the Duke was no longer there. 'Your estate,' she carefully corrected herself. 'It details the groomsmen at the stables, the gardeners, the handymen, the cleaners and bookkeeper, the cook and waiting staff, and all the other staff who are needed around the estate.'

Lucas gulped, and he didn't even pretend to hide it. He flicked through some of the pages. 'Are all of these staff here all of the time?'

Donald shook his head. 'There are a few permanent staff, but Olivia and I are the only ones that stay on site. Some staff are seasonal, some part-time and some sessional.' He went to continue, then also halted his words. 'The former Duke used his cook a few days a week, and she baked for him too. He didn't really like the bother of preparing his own food.'

Lucas held up his hand. 'It's fine,' he said, even though these words seemed strange. 'I have no problem with you both calling my father the Duke; it's how you knew him. I'm not a big person on titles.'

What else could he say? This was all so alien to him. He looked around the kitchen. It didn't matter that it was only one room. It led to a pantry, and a utility room, and what looked like a boot room.

'I can't believe one person owned all this.'

Olivia was twisting her hands together. 'It's been in the family for two hundred years,' she said swiftly. 'And lots of other things happen here. The Duke allowed parts of the house to be used for conferences and weddings. He also hosted a number of dignitaries and guests on behalf of the royal family. He was a huge supporter of a number of charities. Some of the bedrooms are converted to allow guests with disabilities to stay. There's a lift in the left wing, and Costley Hall has regularly been used as a respite facility for families and children. Our event manager takes care of most of these things, and there's also riding lessons from the stables.'

The more he heard, the more he felt swamped.

He was a doctor. Show him a patient—show him the most difficult patient in the world, with the most obscure condition—and Lucas would roll up his sleeves and get to work. But this?

Donald continued. 'Actually, the events manager is anxious to meet you. She wants to check your availability for certain dates and functions.'

Lucas gave a short cough. 'What?'

Skye caught his eye and, under the table, her hand rested on his leg firmly, but even she looked a bit overwhelmed by all this.

'Well, this is all new, of course. And I'm sure Lucas will be able to meet with her, but not today, and not until he's managed to get to grips with his role in the estate.' She gave her brightest smile and Lucas wondered if the others knew it was entirely forced, and on his behalf. 'Remember, he still works full-time at The Harlington and has duties and responsibilities to consider.'

'But you're the Duke now,' said Olivia quickly. 'I'm sure you won't need to bother with being a doctor now. And it really is quite urgent.'

He didn't get a chance to speak because Skye was on her feet, the chair legs screeching on the black and white tiles.

'Well, the estate has managed for the last ten months without a Duke. Lucas will need to decide his own time frames. If you don't mind, we'll go for a look around.'

Olivia spoke immediately. 'The Duke's suite is on the first floor on the left.'

Without wasting another second, Skye reached over and took his hand, keeping the smile on her face as she guided him along the corridor next to her.

CHAPTER FOUR

SKYE WAS DECIDEDLY ignoring the little flashes dancing up her arm as she held Lucas's warm palm and focused on the fact that he was swearing softly under his breath the full length of the corridor.

The swearing didn't stop as she picked a corridor to walk down, glancing from side to side at some rooms before finding one she thought might be suitable, pulling him inside and closing the door firmly behind them both.

To be honest, she was feeling a bit light-headed, and a bit sick—and it was nothing to do with Olivia's cake. It was the enormity of all this. It was all very well finding out Lucas was a duke. The information at the solicitors' had seemed overwhelming, but actually seeing Costley Hall in reality—took things to a whole other level. Lucas seemed so normal. He *was* normal. How would this all change him? All she really knew was that it was a million miles away from where she'd grown up in a council estate in one of the less salubrious parts of London.

The room they'd walked into was a library. It was an exceptionally beautiful room, kitted out in dark wood, lined with rows of bookcases and expensive-looking books, a rolling ladder, a desk and chair, then a fireplace with chesterfield sofas and a dark red rug.

All along one side were wide windows, looking out onto the gardens at the rear and allowing an exceptional amount of light to stream into what would otherwise have been a dark room.

Skye collapsed onto one sofa and waited until Lucas sank into the other. He leaned forward and put his head in his hands, shaking it fiercely. 'No. No way. Absolutely not.'

Skye let him rant. She would have done exactly the same in his shoes, so was in no position to judge.

As they'd sat in the kitchen and asked questions, what had started as a nice introduction had seemed to turn into the biggest list of all time. The expectations of the new Duke were high, and Skye wondered if Lucas might just decide to run for the hills.

She decided to try and play devil's advocate, tamping down her feelings too. 'They seem nice enough,' she said. 'I think they might just have unrealistic expectations of the role you might want to play here.'

He sat up and sighed. She could practically feel the anger emanate from him. 'I don't think I want any role here. The house is beautiful, but why would I actually stay here? I rent a flat in London and that meets my needs. I know nothing about estates, or stables, or how to run a place like this.'

'I get it.' She nodded as she looked around the room, then gave him a cheeky smile. 'But can you just give me five minutes of bliss, please?' She closed her eyes and breathed in heavily.

'Skye, what are you doing?' he asked.

She opened her eyes again and held out her hands. 'Ever since I was tiny, my life's ambition was to have my own library. This place, the smell—' she pointed to the ladder '—that is part of my childhood dream. Look, it's on wheels.' She got up and touched it gently to see if it moved. It stubbornly stayed in one place, so she gave it a tougher shove and it squeaked and moved along the runners at the top and bottom with an uncomfortable noise. Skye ignored it and ran her hand along the spines of the books on the shelves. Red, brown and blue volumes with gold lettering. 'I don't even know what these are,' she said. 'But I want to read them all.' She walked around the room and then she let out a squeak similar to the ladder. 'Oh, look!'

Lucas stood up and wandered over to where she was standing. Her finger was pointing at a large and slightly threadbare pink velvet chaise longue.

'Oh, my,' she said with glee, before positioning herself on it comically. 'I always wanted one of these.'

She laid one hand on her forehead to shield her eyes from the rays of sun that were streaming through the window on this winter's day. After a moment she opened her eyes and said to him, 'Bit of a draught, right enough.'

Lucas laughed and sighed at the same time. 'I appreciate the deflection.' Skye kept smiling at him because he knew exactly what she'd been doing. 'But I imagine this whole house is a bit of a draught. There are probably regulations that say the windows can't be changed.'

'I have a sealant gun,' she said, swinging

her legs off the chaise longue and standing up. They were closer than she'd expected, but he didn't move away. She tilted her head up towards him. 'This whole place is overwhelming, Lucas. Only thing I can say is, don't make any sudden decisions. Like I said, this place has functioned for ten months before they managed to find you and let you know about it. Okay, there will likely be some things outstanding, but I'm sure they can wait a while longer.'

Skye took a breath. Longing to tell him that whilst she found this place a bit magical, she also would likely be scared to touch anything else whilst she was here. And questions were circulating in her head. Would Lucas change, become part of the aristocracy, and next thing she knew he'd be engaged to a princess from somewhere spectacular? It all just seemed too much, but she was determined to keep supporting him, even if she was terrified.

They stayed like that for a few seconds, Skye Carter looking up at him with those bright blue eyes. Her blonde hair was sitting perfectly on her shoulders in a way that wouldn't be allowed in the hospital, and the concern and sincerity in her eyes was genuine.

He knew it instinctively. From the day he'd met her she'd been a genuine soul, with a spark about her. The palm of his hand itched. More than anything, right now he wanted to reach out and touch her. The feelings of attraction he'd been trying to downplay before now—purely because of everything else that was going on for them both—were hard to ignore. As he stood, not moving away, her perfume drifted up around him.

He could picture himself as a child, reading stories about snakes being piped out of a basket by a snake charmer, and that was exactly how he felt.

How would she react if he touched her cheek right now and bent to kiss her? Right now, they were so close they were practically touching, and neither of them seemed inclined to step away. They hadn't talked about taking the next step. Was she waiting for him to make a move?

She blinked, then her phone beeped loudly in her pocket, causing them both to jump. Skye let out a nervous laugh and pulled it out, frowning for a few seconds as she swiped something open and read it.

'Everything okay?' he asked as she finally stepped away and moved closer to the window. On a winter's day like this, the sun was now hidden behind a cloud and the library wasn't well lit.

Her head came up sharply, her expression surprised. 'I... I...' She hesitated, something he wasn't used to seeing in Skye. Her face broke into a smile. 'I've got an interview for a new job.'

His stomach fell. 'You have? Where?'

He couldn't help the first thought that was echoing around his head.

Oh, no. Oh, no. Oh, no.

It didn't matter that it was selfish and pathetic. He genuinely enjoyed working with her, and she was the only person who knew his awkward secret. He wasn't ready for her to step out of his life.

'I told you I'd applied for a few,' she started as he nodded. 'This one is for a practice nurse job in a GP surgery.' She peered out of the window. 'It's in London. But I've applied for another one too, that actually isn't too far from here.'

A tiny wave of relief flowed over him. At least one of the jobs she'd applied for was near here. That was good.

He paused for a second, trying to think

about Skye and not himself. 'You've applied for a few—is this the one that you want?'

She sighed and sat back down on the chaise longue. She shook her head lightly. 'I actually don't know what I want. I just hope that I get invited for an interview somewhere and feel a good vibe. You know how that happens sometimes?'

'Oh, yeah,' he had to agree. 'There have been a few places I've interviewed that I've wanted to walk out five minutes after walking in. Then there are others I get back out to the car and feel jealous of all the people already there.'

'See, you get it,' she said. 'I'm hoping I get that feeling.'

'When's the interview?'

'Next week—know anything about general practice?'

He nodded hesitantly. Even if Skye got the job, she'd still need to work at least a month's notice. He would still see her.

'I have a few friends that have gone into general practice. Want me to ask them what they'd be looking for in a practice nurse?'

Her shoulders visibly relaxed. 'Yes, thanks, that would be great.' She gave a sigh. 'I think I just need to be somewhere different. I've always loved my job and my colleagues, but now, every time I step inside, I remember when I had to go and tell Ross, our boss, about my mum and her diagnosis. And then again when I needed to take time off to nurse her at home.'

He gave a nod of understanding. 'So, you want to make different kinds of memories?'

For a second her eyebrows shot up, and she gave him a mocking look.

He waved his hand. 'You know what I mean.'

She sighed. 'Yes, I do.' She bit her lip. 'Just like you, with this place. You have a chance to make a whole new set of memories here.'

He was just contemplating what she'd said as she started to walk back around the room, running her fingers along the books. 'I'd still love a library some day.' Her smile broadened and she turned back to him. 'Maybe that's the job I should be applying for—a librarian.'

Now it was his turn to laugh. 'You couldn't be an ordinary librarian,' he joked as he took his turn to push the ladder along its rails. 'You'd be the kind of librarian that's in those TV shows. Everyone thinks they're quiet, but they actually have a superhero cape and fight off vampires or have secret rooms that lead into other worlds.'

Skye moved alongside him and raised her eyebrows. 'Are you sure you're a doctor and not a fiction writer?'

He shrugged and smiled. She was definitely making this easier for him. 'Maybe I'm a bit of both?'

'What say we take a good look around?'

He glanced at his watch. 'I think it's going to ice up again soon—not sure we want to stay here too late. The country roads around here probably don't get gritted.'

If she knew he was still feeling a bit out of sorts here she didn't say it, and for a second he thought she might have looked relieved.

'Okay then, what about a quick look around the first floor? We can call it quits after that and come back another day.'

Warmth spread through him. This wasn't just a one-off trip. She intended to come back with him again.

'Sure,' he said quickly and they left the library and walked back to the main entrance-way and up one of the curved sets of stairs. Lucas ran his hand up the dark polished wooden banister as they climbed the wide, red-carpeted stairs.

'I wonder how many people have touched this banister over the years,' he said with a hint of melancholy.

'You should be proud,' she said.

He looked at her in surprise. 'What do you mean?'

'You heard the stories that Donald and Olivia told you. Some people will have been patients, some doctors and nurses, some evacuees.' She glanced up to the dome and smiled. Dark clouds had filled the sky above so the delicate glasswork wasn't quite so visible. 'Think of the stories they could tell. And even the last few years—' she gave him a nudge '—I bet there are a few wedding albums that have a shot of the bride and groom taken from below to get that gorgeous dome in the picture. And if it was like earlier, with the sun streaming through, making it look like confetti was on the walls...' She let her voice trail off, a wistful smile on her face.

'Why do you always look on the bright side?' he asked.

'Is that a cue for a song?' she joked.

He shook his head. 'Just an observation.'

Skye took a deep breath as they headed down one of the corridors, opening doors as they went. 'It's not really my nature. I'm faking it. My mum tried to persuade me it was a better frame of mind to adopt. And I vowed that I'd try.'

There was a hint of wobble in her voice and, before he could think about it, Lucas put an arm around her shoulders. They stopped at one of the doors to peer inside.

'I think that sounds good,' he said gently. 'Your mum was obviously a wise woman.'

She looked up at him with slightly damp eyes. 'She'd like that someone said that about her.'

Lucas stayed silent, giving her a moment to collect herself.

Skye took a kind of shuddery breath, then changed the subject. 'It's a bedroom,' she said.

He gave a short laugh. 'Seems so.'

The wide window let some dim light into the larger than average room, with a double bed, wardrobe, dresser and heavy brocade curtains at the window. The room smelt surprisingly fresh and, after a few sniffs, Skye pointed to the air freshener attached to the plug point. Another door led to a bathroom with bath, sink and toilet all in white, with some rather grand taps. The tiling was a little dated but the room was spotless.

'Do you think they're all like this?' Skye asked.

'I have no idea,' Lucas replied and they walked down the hall, opening more doors and peering into other rooms. The layouts were similar, the décor slightly different. They found what looked like an upstairs drawing room, three times the size of the other rooms, with other versions of chesterfield furniture. There were a few bathrooms, what looked like an office, and a few smaller rooms near the end of the corridor.

Then they came to the rooms that Olivia and Donald had mentioned. They were clearly designed for people with additional needs. Adaptations were in place in the bathrooms, the rooms had more modern furniture, special beds and completely flat floors with no rugs or carpets. There was also a lift near these rooms and Skye pressed the button to call it.

'Sorry,' she said with a shrug. 'I was one of those kids that if you put a sign on something saying *Don't Touch*, guess what I did?'

The lift pinged and opened and they bent forward to look inside. 'Wow, it's big,' said Skye.

Lucas nodded. He was starting to understand a little more about the place. He walked back to one of the rooms and went over to the windows. It really was getting dark now, but he tried to imagine what a respite session here might be like for some of the families that had been mentioned. Most of them had probably never stayed anywhere like this before. He still found it hard to believe that he actually had.

If he didn't get his act together, would all this good work fall by the wayside?

'So many rooms,' said Skye as they stood together. 'I wonder how long it takes to clean this place?'

He smiled. 'Why would that be the first thing that comes into your head?'

She paused as she looked at him, and he wondered if she was adjusting what she really wanted to say. She gave a half-shrug. 'Just thinking in days gone by I'd likely have been a scullery maid in a place like this. Think how long it would take to scrub the floors.'

She sounded kind of strange, so he put his arm back around her shoulders. 'You don't need to scrub floors, and you don't need to clean. Maybe you can give me decorating advice?'

They moved back to the staircase and his

hand paused near a door. It was as if Skye knew exactly why he was hesitating.

'The Duke's suite. Do you want to look inside?'

He couldn't pretend he wasn't curious. So, he pushed open the door. The suite was large. There was a sitting room, a dressing room, a huge bedroom and an equally large bathroom. He couldn't help but look at the slightly dated furnishings and run his finger along the dark wood desk, wondering how often his father had sat here. A man he'd never known.

There was a photo on the bureau that stopped him dead. It was his father, his mother and clearly an infant him on a beach somewhere. How long had that photo been here? Just less than thirty years?

He gulped and took another look around. There was a bright red footstool. An elegant cushioned rocking chair. A rainbow stuffed toy which looked decidedly modern. Another photo, this time of his father and Albert on a golf course somewhere. They were laughing heartily and something about that made him want to ask even more questions.

An impulse grabbed him and he opened a large mahogany cupboard and his breath caught somewhere in his throat. His father's clothes were all still hanging there, and a certain aroma of cologne swept towards him.

He lifted his hand and touched the well-cut suits, obviously from Savile Row, along with designer shirts and ties. There was even what looked like a burgundy velvet smoking jacket. Aside from that, it looked as if his father had been a well-turned-out man.

It was the first real pang that he felt, wishing he had known him.

He walked from room to room and Skye just stood back and let him, not speaking, just letting him have this time.

When he'd finished, he knew his eyes were likely shining with the threat of tears. Skye moved beside him.

'This place is pretty much a mirror image of itself—let's look at the other side.'

They moved across the grand staircase to the other side, and opened the opposite suite. It was clean and tidy, but had a neglected air about it. The furnishings were in keeping with the rest of the house, but without the same lived-in feel or individuality.

'Do you think this was your mother's at one point?'

Lucas gave a sad smile as he ran his finger along the top of a full-length mirror that stood next to the wardrobe. 'Oh, I think so,' he said with irony. 'Even though there's a dressing room next door filled with mirrors, she'd still have to have another in here.'

He took a deep breath. 'If I have to stay at some point, I'll probably use these rooms instead of the Duke's.'

'Instead of your father's,' Skye said gently.

He stood for a moment, letting that sink in.

'Instead of my father's,' he repeated as she slid her hand into his. He knew she was doing it to comfort him. But it took his thoughts to another place. One where Skye wasn't only here as his friend.

The more time he spent with her, the more he was attracted to her. At first, he'd just instantly noticed her good looks and admirable don't-mess-with-me manner. But over the last few weeks, as he'd got to know her better, it was her warmth and empathy that had drawn him in, her sense of humour and intelligence. Even now, she seemed to know exactly what to do in this unforeseen situation.

He swallowed, his throat instantly dry.

'Hey, you.' Skye gave a squeeze of his hand. 'Is it time to go?'

Lucas gave a grateful shrug. His head was spinning.

They headed back down the stairs and made their way back to the kitchen. Donald had vanished but Olivia was pacing. She jumped as they walked back in.

'Thanks for letting us have a look around,' Lucas said graciously. 'But it's getting dark and we're going to head back to London.'

'You're not staying?' She seemed genuinely surprised.

He shook his head. 'I'm working again tomorrow. We have to get back.'

He could only describe the look on Olivia's face as disappointed, and he didn't really understand.

'If you could give me your phone number, I'll be in touch when we're going to come back.' Saying 'we' made him feel strangely comfortable.

She pulled open a drawer and brought out a card with the former Duke's details on it, a line drawing of Costley Hall with the address and phone number underneath.

'We can get these changed,' she said apologetically.

He shook his head and stroked the card for the briefest of seconds. 'It's fine, honestly. We'll talk about it some other time.'

Olivia followed them to the main door and

watched them climb into the car, which was covered in a dusting of snow. Lucas started the engine—or at least he tried to start the engine. It turned but didn't catch.

Skye gave him an anxious glance. 'Maybe it's just the cold?'

He tried again; this time the car was silent.

They sat and looked at each other for a few moments, neither of them wanting to say the words out loud.

Skye pulled a face. 'Sorry, don't have any roadside cover.'

Lucas closed his eyes for a second. 'Me neither.' He looked back out at Costley Hall. 'Or maybe they would expect home start from here.'

Both jumped as there was a small knock at the window. Olivia was shivering outside. Lucas opened his door.

'Car trouble?' she asked.

He nodded to the obvious question and climbed out.

'Would you like to borrow a car?' she asked.

Lucas felt his heart leap in his chest. 'You have something I could borrow?'

'Well, it wouldn't be borrowing, exactly.

Because they're all yours. They were your father's cars. He was a bit of a collector.'

Skye shot him a hopeful look.

'I have cars?'

Olivia shivered again, and Lucas remembered himself. 'You should get back inside.' She nodded gratefully and they followed her back into the house.

'Give me a moment,' she said, then disappeared down the back corridor.

'I thought for a minute we were going to be stranded here,' said Skye with a relieved smile. 'Thank goodness there is another car.'

Footsteps echoed along the corridor and Donald appeared in a thick jacket. He gave a nod. 'Come with me, Your Grace.'

Lucas didn't think it was the time to object to the title and they both followed Donald through the dark corridors and out through a door at the back on the right-hand side of the house. It led directly into another dark space, and after a few moments Donald flicked a switch.

Lucas held his breath. The garage was the size of a football pitch and it was filled with a variety of cars, some with gleaming bodywork and some covered and hidden from view. Rolls-Royces, Bentleys, Aston Martins, Mercedes, BMWs in a variety of ages and styles. He gulped. It was like a teenage boy's fantasy.

Donald gave him a few moments, obviously realising this would be some kind of shock.

Lucas's voice came out slightly higher-pitched than normal. 'You didn't mention cars before, Donald.'

The burly man turned and gave a slight bow. 'You didn't need one then, Your Grace.'

Skye started to move. Lucas wasn't sure how much she knew about cars, but her eyes were wide as she ran her fingers lightly along a few of the bonnets and wings.

'How many are there?' she asked.

'Thirty-three,' said Donald smartly. 'The Duke loved his cars, but he reduced his collection over the last few years. He also allowed a few select friends to drive his cars.'

Lucas shivered. 'Was one of those friends Albert Cunningham?'

'Oh, no,' said Skye, her hand going to her mouth. 'The Aston Martin was one of the Duke's cars?'

'What happened to the Aston Martin?' asked Donald with one eyebrow raised.

'We'll talk about it later,' said Lucas with

a wave of his hand. He still couldn't take his eyes off the cars in front in him.

Donald gave a brief nod. 'Which one do you want? I'll get you the keys.'

Lucas blinked. Was that a DeLorean back there? A Ferrari? And if these were on display, what was beneath the covers?

He took a breath. 'I need something that can handle country roads, possibly ice, and we're going back to London, so really I need something that car thieves won't track in the blink of an eye.' He smiled and shook his head. 'Do you have anything normal in here? Something that I can drive in London, where I won't need to worry about dings and scratches?'

This time both eyebrows went up and Donald gestured for them to follow him, going to a safe on the wall and keying in some numbers before pulling out a set of car keys. He threaded his way through the cars and moved over to a gleaming black Range Rover with shaded windows.

'It's top of the range,' said Donald matter-of-factly. 'The Duke wouldn't buy anything less, but it can certainly handle country roads, ice and whatever else is thrown at it.'

'It has *Steal Me* written all over it,' sighed Skye with a smile.

Lucas nodded, then stopped. 'Wait a minute—what about insurance?'

Donald shook his head. 'All the cars are insured under the Costley Hall estate. You're covered to drive it.'

Lucas glanced at the keys in his hand. 'You're sure?'

Donald nodded and folded his arms. 'I still want to know about the Aston Martin.'

Lucas gave a slightly nervous smile. 'Sure, when I get back.'

Donald moved over and flicked another switch and one of the garage doors glided open. Lucas and Skye climbed into the luxurious car, starting the engine and sinking down into the already warming leather seats.

Skye looked at the lights on the dashboard and laughed. 'It's like the Starship Enterprise in here.'

Lucas nodded and moved a few switches to make the lights and windscreen wipers automatic. 'Ready to head back to London?'

She took a deep breath and stared at him for a few moments, her blue eyes fixed on his. 'Thanks,' she said simply.

'What for?' he asked. 'It's you that's been helping me.'

As he moved the car outside the garage and gave a wave to Donald, she wrapped her arms around herself, waiting for the car to heat up. 'No, I think it's pretty equal,' she countered.

'What do you mean?' The driveway was snow-encrusted now and driving along it was like taking a trip through a winter wonderland.

She kept rubbing her arms even though the temperature was rising rapidly.

'All of this,' she said in a quiet voice. 'I know it's a lot, and I know you're overwhelmed by it all, but for me?' She looked at him with sorrow in her eyes. 'I don't mean to be selfish, but it's a distraction. One that I needed.' She looked guilty for a second. She took a juddery breath. 'Going back to work has helped. But every morning, when I wake up, for a few brief moments I feel normal, and then I remember that my mum died and it all crashes back.' Tears slid down her cheeks. 'I should be over this. I should be coping better with this. I got to nurse my mum the way I wanted to, I've had time to sort out all the accounts, the house stuff, and all her things.'

Lucas was trying to keep his eyes on the

road but there was no way he could do that when Skye was clearly crying. He looked for a suitable place to pull over and did so sharply, cutting the engine, turning to face her and unfastening their seatbelts. It only took him a few seconds to pull her into his arms.

'I should be better than this,' she sobbed against him, her warm breath filtering through to his chest. He held her close, stroking the back of her hair and whispering reassuring words. Guilt was sweeping over him. He'd known about her bereavement. Her fellow staff members had warned him to treat her carefully. But because she seemed so self-assured, so strong, it hadn't occurred to him it might all be a front.

Skye was caring and compassionate with patients, and her years in A&E had clearly taught her to take no prisoners. He'd liked that about her. It had been the first thing he'd noticed about her, and the feisty attitude was definitely part of the attraction.

But what if that really wasn't Skye? What if it was just a work persona? He hated to admit he'd been leaning on her throughout all this. She'd been great and had stayed by his side, but all the while she'd been falling apart inside.

'Who says there's a timeline on grief?' he said softly. 'I'm sorry I haven't asked more. I'm sorry I've been relying on you so much when I should have been a better friend. This was your mum, Skye. You've had a whole lifetime with her. You had routines with her. It doesn't go away at once. No matter how hard you try.'

She sniffed and lifted her head, letting him see her tear-filled blue eyes. 'I'm sorry.' She shook her head and pushed herself away from him. The sudden space between them felt cold and empty.

'Skye, I hope by this point you'd consider us friends. You can talk to me, tell me how you're feeling. If you're having a bad day, you should say so. We didn't need to come here today—we could have done something else. Something you wanted to do.'

'But that's just it—' she blinked '—I *did* want to come here. I wanted to be with you. I wanted the distraction. Everything at home, and at work, just tells me I need to look at my life and make a fresh start.'

Lucas took a deep breath. He couldn't pretend he didn't feel guilty.

'Skye, a distraction might be fine. But the trouble was, I got to Costley Hall and just felt overwhelmed by it all. I stopped paying attention to you. My brain was trying to understand how much it costs to heat a place like that, and to keep the businesses and land running. I feel as if I'm not cut out for all this.' He put his hand on his chest. 'I trained as a doctor, not as a duke. I'm not sure I want to spend the time and energy that this will take.'

He reached over and brushed the side of her cheek for the briefest of seconds. 'When what I should be doing is looking after the first friend that I met when I got here.'

There was something there. A definite spark between them. His brain was telling him that now was not the time to act on it. But even as he was looking at her the edges of her lips tilted upwards. Her head moved a little closer and she reached up towards him.

'Thank you,' she breathed, resting her forehead against his.

They stayed in that position for a few moments. He wanted to reach out and take one of her hands and hold it in his. But he also wanted to respect her. They were on a dark, snowy country road. He didn't want to make a move that could make her feel compromised. He'd never do that. Every cell in his body was aware of the breathing rhythm of their bodies that had automatically synched with each other.

'Any time,' he whispered back, and she smiled, before eventually lifting her head and settling back into her seat.

Lucas took the cue and restarted the engine, the windscreen wipers coming on automatically. The snow was falling thick and fast.

Skye peered out into the pitch-black night. 'It's beginning to look a lot like Christmas,' she joked. Then her gaze flicked back to him. 'There's a thought. I didn't see a Christmas tree or decorations in Costley Hall.'

He frowned. 'Come to think of it, I didn't either. I wonder why?' As he steered the car carefully along the twisting roads, he gave a sigh. 'I actually prefer New Year to Christmas. I always offer to work Christmas Day.'

'Me too,' said Skye in surprise. 'Or maybe it's just that I'm not married and don't have kids, so I've always chosen to volunteer to do Christmas to let my colleagues with families have the time off.'

'When did you last have a Christmas off?' he asked.

She shook her head. 'Never. Since I was a student nurse, I've always offered to work. My mum and I used to have Christmas dinner on another day. And I'd just record anything special I wanted to watch from Christmas Day.' She gave him a curious glance. 'Don't you spend Christmas or New Year with your mum?'

'My mum?' he said with amusement in his voice. 'Ever since I was at medical school, my mother has endeavoured to get herself an exotic Christmas and New Year invite—usually to a private island somewhere. I told you, not your typical mother.'

'And you never get an invite?' she asked incredulously.

He laughed out loud. 'Never mind *me* not getting an invite. Half the time I'm quite sure my mother *didn't* get an invite.'

Skye laughed in surprise. 'You're joking?'

He shook his head as the sign ahead indicated the way back to London. 'You haven't met her. You'll understand when you do.'

'I think you mean she hasn't met *me* yet,' said Skye. 'I'm more than a match for your mother.' She was joking—he knew she was—but after a long and stressful day, she still had the ability to make him smile.

'Can't wait to see when that happens,' he responded. 'I definitely want a ringside seat.'

She raised her eyebrows. 'Want to take bets on whether Mr Cunningham might want one too?'

They'd joined the main road into London.

'Ah, the mysterious Mr Cunningham.' Lucas gave a slow nod. 'By all accounts, he's doing a lot better now.' He gave Skye a sideways glance. 'Maybe it's time to go and see him again, this time to talk about Costley Hall.'

Skye nodded in response. 'Your mission, if you choose to accept it…' She let her voice tail off.

'Wanna come with me when I go?' he asked.

'Absolutely,' she replied without hesitation. 'There's no show without Punch.'

He smiled as a warm feeling spread through him. There was no question that he absolutely wanted her to be by his side. But in the capacity of a friend—or something more?

CHAPTER FIVE

SKYE KEPT HER eyes on the board, scanning constantly to try and keep her A&E department viable.

She moved to the desk. 'We have four ambulances that can't unload patients. Every bed and trolley in here is being used. Time for a huddle. Call the emergency page holder.'

She gave a signal and the A&E internal emergency lights flashed twice. They were strategically placed around the department and used for a variety of reasons. An emergency huddle was one of them.

She gave it five minutes, until most of her staff were present, before she started. She could sense Lucas before she even saw him. He came up behind her, the smell of his aftershave instantly recognisable. It was strange how the scent of someone could do strange things to a person.

She could remember the first time she'd noticed it and thought it kind of nice. After the first few times, she'd started to associate it directly with Lucas. Then, after a few weeks, it had started to make her skin tingle and her stomach flutter. Whilst what was going on in Lucas's life was proving a distraction from her own issues, the man himself was enough of a distraction without the prospect of him being a duke being thrown into the equation.

He'd been so nice last week when she'd had a mini meltdown in his car. It had been a long day and things had just seemed to pile up and overwhelm her. It was uncommon for Skye, but then she'd never been in a position like this before.

Dev, the page holder, appeared and Skye gave a nod. 'Right, everyone, we need to clear some room in A&E. We have four ambulances that need to unload, patients we need to treat. Ro, update me on your patients.'

'I have two patients with chest X-ray films to be reported, both elderly, both probable chest infections and both requiring admission to medicine. I also have two Paed patients who can probably go home with medicines, but I can't get a paed down here to see them.'

'I'm waiting on Surgical,' sighed Louise,

another staff member. 'Three patients waiting to be seen.'

'Ortho for me,' said Adam. 'The plaster room is backed up. Hopefully not for much longer. I've six patients waiting on some kind of cast.'

Skye gave a nod. Adam could put a plaster cast on with expertise and quicker than most people could drink a cup of coffee. She knew all her staff were working as hard as possible.

Lucas spoke next. 'I have four drunk and disorderly patients. All with a variety of minor injuries, but none of whom are fit to be safely discharged as yet.'

Skye looked at Dev, whose job was to manage all the beds in the hospital. He had considerable sway, because a hospital with all beds full was a hospital that would have to close to admissions. It was the biggest 'no' that existed in healthcare.

'Tell all specialties that if they aren't down here in the next five minutes we'll be assessing their patients and admitting direct to their wards,' Skye said with a no argument kind of voice. 'Lucas, the two paeds…can you assess and, if safe, send them on their way? And Dev, can you find me a healthcare support worker and an area for our four drunk and disorderly patients to be observed for the next couple of hours?'

She turned back and leaned over the desk. 'I'm going to phone Radiology now and ask for reports on those two chest X-rays.' Then she nodded to one of her ANPs. 'Leigh, please go and assess the patients in the ambulances. If any are urgent, let us know, and we'll clear an area.'

The staff all nodded and walked away quickly. No one liked it when the department was like this. It didn't feel safe for staff or patients, and Skye wasn't prepared to compromise on the care they delivered.

A few minutes later—with a promise of X-ray reports in the next ten minutes, and a few scowls from specialty doctors who'd arrived in A&E—she went to join Lucas with the paediatric patients.

He looked up as she walked in, and handed her a tablet. 'Skye, this is Mikey and his mum Caroline.'

Skye gave them both a smile. Mum was already wrestling Mikey back into his clothes.

'Mikey has a chest infection and I've prescribed some antibiotics for him. Can you ask someone to supply?'

She nodded and signalled to another nurse

walking past. The hospital pharmacy was closed at night, but the most commonly used prescriptions were pre-prepared for supply in A&E. All they needed was the patient's name, and some instructions given.

With a few words of goodbye, Skye and Lucas moved into the other cubicle with the second paediatric patient. As they walked through the curtains the tiny baby in her mother's arms vomited.

Skye moved quickly to assist and her heart skipped a few beats when she saw the colour of the vomit. She looked at the tablet that Lucas had picked up. *Esther Lewis, ten days old, vomiting and excessive crying. Colic. For assessment.*

She turned over the cloth she'd just wiped Esther's face with.

Lucas moved quickly. 'Do you mind if I examine Esther?' he asked her mother, taking the squealing baby and gently laying her on the trolley, before examining her with the tenderest of touches. Little Esther had slight abdominal distension, but as soon as Lucas brushed his fingers against her little belly she squealed. He fastened her to the nearest monitor, which showed a rapid heart rate to match her rapid breathing.

Skye put her arm around mum. She knew the next set of questions.

Esther's mum, Juliette, was in her early twenties. 'It is something, isn't it? My friends thought I was overreacting.'

Skye put her hand over Juliette's as Lucas asked a few questions about feeding and nappies. 'You're not overreacting, Juliette. You're in the right place. We can look after Esther.'

Lucas sat down in the chair opposite. 'I'm so glad you came in, Juliette. I think Esther has a condition called volvulus. It's when the bowel twists so the blood supply gets cut off.' He lifted the cloth and opened it to show Juliette the green bile. 'Is this the first time Esther's vomit has been like this?'

Juliette's eyes widened. 'Yes, it's just been milk up until now.'

He nodded. 'Then all your instincts were spot-on. This is a sign of volvulus. Right now, Esther can't absorb and digest her milk the way she should. I'm going to get a paediatric surgeon to come down right now and do some emergency tests, but it's likely Esther will need surgery in the next few hours. Can I phone someone to come and join you?'

Skye felt Juliette sag against her.

'Surgery? But she's only ten days old. She

can't have surgery.' Her voice was rising in panic.

Lucas stood up and gave Skye a nod. 'Will you be okay for a few minutes while I go and make the calls?'

Skye nodded and wrapped Esther loosely in a blanket, handing her back to Juliette to hold for a few minutes.

'She'll be fine. I know she's tiny, and that she's your whole world. Our surgeons will come and explain everything to you. They've done this operation a number of times. This condition can affect up to one in three thousand babies, boys and girls. Often, they have to do this on preemie babies that are only around twenty-four or twenty-six weeks gestation. Dr Hastings will come back in a few minutes and he'll slip a little needle into Esther's arm so we can keep her hydrated.' She rubbed Juliette's back. 'Now, can I call someone for you?'

Juliette nodded and swiped open her phone with trembling hands. 'Here,' she said. 'Can you call my mum and dad?'

'Absolutely,' she replied as Lucas walked back in. 'That was quick.'

'Mr Amjad has just finished another case.

He's coming along with Claire, the anaesthetist.'

Skye kept the phone in one hand as she pulled over a small trolley with the other, placing the equipment on it that he needed to slip in an IV.

He gave her a nod. 'Let me make a call and I'll be straight back.'

Skye couldn't help but think they made a good team as she quickly spoke to Juliette's mum and dad, who were shocked but said they would be at The Harlington soon.

Within an hour, all Esther's tests were completed, the diagnosis confirmed, and Skye walked the family along to the waiting room at Theatre, supplying them with some tea and biscuits for their wait.

By the time she got back to A&E, the ambulances had cleared and there were five free cubicles. Adam had cleared the plaster room, three patients were waiting on porters to take them up to wards, and the four drunk and disorderly patients had been transferred to another area where all were being observed.

A huge box of twenty-four doughnuts was sitting in the middle of the nurses' station near the centre of A&E.

'I think this is coffee time,' said Lucas, glancing at his watch.

Skye took another quick check around to make sure everyone was okay, picking up a note on the desk for Lucas. 'I agree,' she said, lifting a napkin and selecting her favourite raspberry iced doughnut.

They walked along to the staffroom after Lucas selected a doughnut of his own, then made coffee simultaneously next to each other.

Skye let out a laugh. 'We're like an old married couple.'

Lucas waggled a spoon at her. 'If you touch my doughnut, I want a divorce.'

They sank into the nearby seats and Lucas opened the note that had been left for him. He looked thoughtful and handed it to Skye. It was from the charge nurse on the ward that Mr Cunningham was due to be discharged from in the next few days.

Heard you were on duty tonight. Just to let you know Mr Cunningham is a poor sleeper and likes to chat. I know you want to speak to him again, so if you get a chance come along. Fran

Skye took a bite of her doughnut. 'Well,

there's an offer you can't really refuse. It might give you a chance to get some answers.'

He nodded thoughtfully. She could see a world of questions and doubts on his face. Was he anxious about asking the questions and what he might find out? Part of her wondered if this might make him more determined not to take over all the duties that went along with being a duke.

'Will you come with me?' he asked. 'There's no show without Punch,' he added with a smile.

She couldn't help the answering smile that spread across her face. 'I think we might have some time,' she agreed. 'Do you think Albert might like a doughnut?'

The lights were dim in the corridor as they made their way to the ward where Albert Cunningham was still a patient, Skye carrying a doughnut on a plate.

The nurse at the station looked up and smiled as she was typing some notes on the computer. 'Are you Dr Hastings?' she asked as they approached.

He nodded, 'And this is Skye Carter, the charge nurse from A&E.'

The nurse gave a nod. 'I'm Allie. Fran said

she'd invited you to pop along. I've just made Albert a cup of tea. He's in good spirits, and once he's assessed as safe on the stairs, he'll be discharged home. You can go and see him—he's in the side room around the corner so he can watch TV through the night.'

'Thanks,' said Lucas, then paused a second. 'How did he do on the stairs?' He could tell from the way the nurse had phrased her response that Albert had already been assessed.

She gave a shrug. 'He's still too unsteady. The physio won't let him be discharged until she judges him safe. She's coming back tomorrow, so we'll see what she says.'

Lucas gave a nod. 'Thanks,' before heading down the corridor with Skye at his side.

'You ready for this?' she asked.

'Probably not,' he admitted. 'But it might be the only time I get a version of the truth, so let's go.'

He knocked gently on the already open door. Albert Cunningham was sitting upright in bed, supported by pillows and watching the flickering TV in the corner of the room. He took a few seconds to recognise Lucas, then waved them in, picking up the remote to silence the television.

'Your Grace.' He nodded, and Lucas felt his skin prickle.

He gave a small smile. 'I honestly can't get used to that,' he admitted. 'I keep wanting to look over my shoulder to see if people are talking to someone else.'

Albert smiled, and his eyes had a wicked twinkle in them—something Lucas hadn't had the chance to see the first time they'd met.

Skye sat down and reached over and touched Albert's hand. 'I'm Skye, I work in A&E with Lucas. I was there when you were brought in. In fact—' she glanced at Lucas '—it was our first night working together. So it's nice to see you looking so much better.' She handed over the plate. 'Here, we brought you a doughnut to go with that cup of tea.'

Albert lifted the paper napkin on the plate and looked in approval at the chocolate iced doughnut. 'Perfect pick,' he complimented. 'Thank you so much, and for your care when I was in A&E.'

'You're welcome.' Skye smiled, settling back into her chair.

Lucas took a breath. He was fortunate that he'd already had his first conversation with

Albert, but he hadn't really asked him anything about Costley Hall or his father.

'We went to visit Costley Hall,' he started.

Albert paused mid bite of his doughnut. He set it down on the plate. 'What did you think?' He was trying to hide it, but there was pride in his voice.

Lucas had to be honest. 'It's a beautiful place, but I'm just not sure what I'm supposed to do with it.'

Albert took a bite of his doughnut and chewed with a few nods, as if he were contemplating what to say.

'And my car wouldn't start, so Donald gave me a loan,' said Lucas, humour in his voice.

'What did you pick?' Albert asked without hesitation.

'It was snowing. I had to be practical. We picked a Range Rover. It's beautiful. So easy to drive.'

Albert blinked. 'I was devastated when I heard about the Aston Martin.' He sighed. 'Your father loved that car. Have you heard anything from the police?'

Lucas shook his head. 'Nothing, I'm afraid.'

Albert shook his head too. 'I'm an old fool. I should never have brought it that day. It was in a James Bond movie,' he said, casting a glance at Skye.

She nodded. 'I know. The police mentioned they thought it was likely stolen by some chancers, but has probably now been sold on to a collector, once they realised what they had.'

Albert leaned back against his pillows, a forlorn expression on his face. 'It's such a beauty. London used to feel a much safer place.'

Lucas waited a few moments and then tried to steer the conversation back to Costley Hall. 'I met Donald and Olivia. I'm assuming that for the last few months everyone has been paid as they should?'

Albert's head tilted to one side. He was astute. That much was crystal-clear. 'Of course,' he said quickly.

Lucas gave a slow nod before he met Albert's gaze. 'So, you can see what I do. I'm a doctor, not a duke. I don't see a role for me at Costley Hall. Everyone seems to have managed for the last ten months without any problems. Can things continue the way they are?'

Albert's gaze narrowed, and Lucas felt his heart sink.

'We didn't get a chance to talk before my

accident.' His words were clipped. 'I'm not sure what my partners have covered with you, but I'll be frank because I owe it to your father. I've looked after much of the estate for the last ten months. But I'm not in any condition to keep doing that, and you absolutely cannot trust my colleagues at the firm.'

Skye gave a shocked gasp, then laughed. 'Say it like you see it, Albert.'

His head turned to her. 'Have you met them?'

She nodded.

'Did you like them?'

'Not for a second,' she admitted.

His face broke into a half smile. 'That's what I like about nurses. They tend to be able to see through the veneer.'

Lucas didn't like how this was going. 'So, what does that mean?'

Albert met his gaze again. 'It means that once I introduce you to your accountant, you'll have to take over.'

Lucas shook his head. 'But I can't—and I'm not sure I want to.'

'Why on earth not?' The incredulity in his tone surprised Lucas and he could see Skye trying to hide a smile.

He took a breath. He wasn't sure what to

make of Albert. Was he the family lawyer? His father's best friend? Or something else?

'Albert, you and my father knew of my existence. But I never knew of yours. I know nothing about being a duke or running an estate. I've spent my whole life dreaming of being a doctor, and completing my training.' He pointed to the floor. 'This is where I want to be.'

Albert looked at him as though he'd spoken in another language. 'But you've seen Costley Hall, you've seen the grounds, the cars, and met the staff. It's a home and lifestyle that millions would beg for, and you don't want it?'

Albert was getting angry now. Lucas didn't want to upset the elderly man, but equally he wasn't going to be pushed into something that a few weeks ago he'd known nothing about.

'You have duties, responsibilities,' Albert continued, but Lucas cut in.

'Exactly, I have duties and responsibilities here.'

Albert's head swivelled and his gaze fixed on Skye. The tone of his voice changed completely. 'Is this because of you?' he asked.

Colour flared in Skye's cheeks, but she wasn't flustered. Instead, she looked Albert straight in the eye. 'I don't think it's because of me,' she answered simply, 'because I'm planning on leaving. I'm not keeping Lucas here.'

'That's not fair, Albert,' said Lucas quickly. 'Skye's here because she's my friend.' The primal urge to protect her came out of nowhere.

Albert looked back to Skye. 'You're leaving the hospital?'

She nodded. 'That's my plan. I have one interview for a job as a practice nurse in a GP surgery in London, and one for the district nursing course.' She glanced over at Lucas. 'And I have another interview, for a GP practice near Costley Hall. I just heard about that one,' she added.

Lucas's heart clenched in his chest. Of course, it didn't matter. Of course, he wanted her to be happy, and of course, he should support his friend in her career choices. But the thought of working here and not having Skye alongside him made him ache in a way that didn't match the fact that he'd only known her for a month or so.

He hadn't known about the interview for the job near Costley Hall, and he couldn't pretend it didn't give him a huge wave of relief, but why? He hadn't even agreed he would do anything with the place. Why did he want her to be near there?

He looked down at his watch. 'We should get back,' he said, rising to his feet.

Albert gave a little jolt. 'But we've not finished.'

'I have to get back to work, Albert. Patients are depending on us.'

Skye stood up too and straightened her tunic.

'You have to take over, Lucas. The will is detailed about your responsibilities, those for the title and the estate.' Albert looked out at the dark night sky. 'It's December already. You have to be ready for the New Year's ball.'

Lucas had already started to make his way to the door. He turned back. 'What?'

Albert had an air of panic about him. 'For the last fifty years there has always been a New Year's ball at Costley Hall. It's a giant fundraiser. It usually brings in around fifty per cent of the income for the charities that the Duke supported. It's vital that it takes place. The plans are already in place. Haven't you spoken to Brianna, the events manager? She spends months getting every detail right.'

'Lucas?' Skye asked quietly, her blue eyes fixing on him.

'I think she might have emailed a few times,' he admitted. 'I just haven't had a chance to read them properly.'

'You have to do it,' said Albert, a pleading tone in his voice. 'It's a tradition. And the charities depend on it.'

Lucas felt himself wavering. 'I'll get in touch with her,' he finally relented before excusing himself.

He walked back down the corridor with Skye, stopping as they turned a corner and looking at his watch again. His head was swimming and he had a sudden feeling of claustrophobia, even though they were in the middle of a long corridor.

This place was just too enclosed. Like all hospitals, it had that aroma about it. Disinfectant. Body fluids. Age. Staleness. Death.

Air. He needed air.

'We have around five minutes,' he said, taking a quick look around, opening a nearby door and ducking inside.

'What on earth are you doing?' asked Skye as she followed him inside.

It was one of the laundry rooms, stocked

with sheets, pillowcases, towels, blankets and scrubs for staff.

There was a small window at the other end and Lucas picked his way over the variety of objects on the floor before he reached it and pushed it upwards, letting in a gust of cold December air.

He stuck his head outside and breathed heavily, trying to suck in the chilly air. He felt a rustle beside him, and then Skye's body along the side of his, and her head stuck out next to his.

'Okay,' she said. 'What are we doing? And, whatever it is, it's too bloody cold.' She grinned at him. 'Did I sound Scottish?'

He laughed, and as he did it was like a shake of relief. For all the craziness that was going on in the world all around him, he still had this friend by his side.

'If you want to sound Scottish,' he said, 'then you have to try and say a lot of special words.'

'Like what?' she asked, her breath steaming the air between them. Her eyes and blonde hair were reflecting the orange light of the lamp-post across the street, giving her a warm amber glow.

'Murr…durr…' he started with.

She laughed and copied him. 'Muhurr... durr,' she tried.

'Drookit,' he said next.

Her brow furrowed. 'Drookit,' she mimicked. 'What is that?'

'Very wet. Mauchit.'

The furrow deepened. 'You're making these up now, aren't you?'

He shook his head, 'It kind of goes hand in hand with the last one usually. Try it. Mauchit.'

Her nose wrinkled. 'Mauch...it.'

'It means very dirty.'

Skye looked confused. 'Very wet and very dirty?'

He grinned. 'Remember the weather in Scotland is different from London. When I lived there, we used to say it was common to see four seasons in one day. I'd go out with a friend to play and it would be blazing sunshine. Four hours later, it had rained, sometimes sleeted too. We'd come back and my friend's granny would complain we were drookit and mauchit, and usually a lot more besides.' He gave her a nudge with his elbow. 'She was really a bit crabbit.'

Now Skye laughed. 'Now, that one I do

know. Crabbit. I know a few people I could put on that list.'

He looked at her sideways. 'Am I on that list?'

She gave him a careful stare, then licked her lips and drew back inside.

Lucas pulled back in too. It really was cold out there and the scrubs that they both wore were no match for the cold weather.

Skye hadn't moved away from him. They were only a few inches apart. She rubbed her cold arms. 'Just depends,' she said softly, with a twinkle in her eyes.

There it was again. That glimmer in the air between them. The one he hadn't yet acted on. Would now be the time he would finally take that step?

His voice was low. 'Depends on what?'

She gave a soft smile. 'You know—the time, the place, the patients.'

He stared at her for the longest time. She'd tried to pin her hair up again, and a few unruly strands had escaped to frame her face. She had some make-up on, making her eyelashes longer and her lips peachy pink. But the colour in her cheeks had come from the air outside. It gave her a glow that just seemed to light her up.

'So, what if the time was night and the place was somewhere magnificent?'

'Like a grand old house that secretly looks a bit like a castle?'

He smiled. 'I might know one of those.'

A smile kept teasing the edges of her lips. Even though they weren't touching, he could feel the heat from her body. It was practically reaching out and filling the gap between them.

'Maybe I don't need a grand old house,' she said.

His skin prickled, and it was nothing to do with the still open window.

'How about I tempt you with a linen closet in one of the oldest, and probably haunted, hospitals in London?'

'Are we still talking about being crabbit?' she asked.

He leaned forward. 'I think we're talking about something else entirely,' he whispered.

Skye tilted her head up towards his, reaching her hands up around his neck.

His lips met hers. It was almost as if something flared in him. She tasted sweet. Just the way he'd imagined she would. One of his hands rested on her hip and the other wound its way into her hair, ruining whatever was left of her clipped-up style.

Skye's body pressed against his, the thin scrubs allowing him to feel the curve of her breasts against his chest. Every part of him was yelling inside, his senses overcome.

He couldn't remember ever feeling a connection like this. There had been plenty of kisses in his past. Plenty of flirtations, plenty of short-term relationships.

But none had the inevitability of this one. The glances. The looks. The feeling.

The getting-to-know-you part. He'd wondered if they'd continue to tiptoe around the friend scenario, when his brain was going in another direction entirely, but, thankfully, it seemed as if Skye's thoughts had moved in the same way.

Everything about this felt right. In all the wrong ways. Especially when they were both working, and currently in a linen closet.

He stepped her back against the stacked rails. There was nowhere for them to go. No table to perch on. Only shelves and shelves of supplies.

Skye arched her back as he ran some kisses down her neck and throat. She let out a strangled gasp and started to laugh, just as his fingers snaked into the gap between her scrubs and made contact with her skin.

She laughed and pressed both hands on his shoulders and gently pushed him back while catching her breath.

Lucas started to laugh too, adjusting his scrubs.

She leaned over and pushed the window back down into place with a bang that made both of them jump.

'How to get caught making out in the hospital,' joked Lucas under his breath.

'I'm not getting caught—' Skye laughed as she eyed his scrubs '—but you'd better wait a few minutes.'

'Hey,' he said, reaching out and taking her hand. 'Thank you.'

'For what?'

'For stopping me screaming out of a hospital window.' He raised his eyebrows. 'It might have attracted some attention.'

She gave a cheeky nod. 'So, *that's* what we were doing?'

He sighed as he smiled. 'That's what I would have been doing if you hadn't been with me.'

Their hands were still entwined. 'I'm glad I could distract you.'

'Oh, you certainly did that.'

For a few moments they just stood there, looking at each other. It was the strangest sensation. But Lucas didn't want the moment to end. Right now, it was just him and her, here at work, where they could just be the doctor and nurse that their patients and colleagues expected.

No pressure. No expectations.

'We'd better get back,' said Skye. 'Let me go first.'

He gave a nod.

As she reached for the handle of the door, she turned and gave him a final glance. 'You can teach me more Scottish words later,' she said with a wink, before she disappeared out of the door.

CHAPTER SIX

HER PHONE BEEPED annoyingly and then rang.

Skye sat straight up in bed. The only person who would phone her at this time was her mother.

It took a few seconds for realisation to swamp her like a tidal wave. It couldn't be her mum. Her mum was gone.

So, who could be calling her?

Her brain started to shift into gear. A major incident at the hospital. That was the only reason she would get a call.

She answered immediately. 'Skye Carter.'

'Major incident alert at The Harlington. Please report for duty.'

It wasn't a real voice. The call was automated, but Skye was out of bed, stripping off her pyjamas and pressing the remote on the TV to see if anything was reported as she dressed.

She washed her face, brushed her teeth and pulled on her scrubs in under three minutes. By the time she was sticking her feet into her trainers she could see the yellow ticker tape line scrolling along the bottom of the news feed.

Train derailment in London. Major incident alert.

Her heart sank like a stone as she grabbed her bag and headed to the door. There wasn't time to watch the rest of the news to see where the incident had occurred.

As she jogged along the street it was still dark. The pavements glistened with frost. The roads had pink, purple and green fluorescence, as if oil had been spilled, but likely meant that ice had formed on them.

It would soon be Christmas. Skye couldn't help but fret over how many families' lives might be about to change because of this major incident.

As she reached the crossroads at the bottom of her street, someone gave a wave and stopped their car. Skye opened the passenger door and climbed in gratefully.

Julie, a radiologist, lived about a mile away and had clearly been called in too. 'Should have called you,' said Julie as soon as she pulled the car away again. 'Haven't really woken up yet though.'

'Me neither,' said Skye. 'Heard anything else?'

Julie shook her head. 'Feeling a bit sick to be truthful. Figured I wouldn't turn the radio on in case it was full of rumours. I'll just get a briefing when I get there.'

Skye's phoned beeped again and she pulled it out of her pocket.

Need me to come and get you?

It was Lucas. All staff had been called. She texted quickly back.

Got a lift, see you there.

Julie shot her a glance. 'Hospital?'

Skye shook her head and answered without thinking. 'One of the docs offering me a lift. He lives really close to The Harlington.'

The words seemed to wake Julie up. 'Lucas Hastings?'

Skye looked at her in surprise. 'How do you know that?'

Julie laughed. 'There's been rumours about

you two for the past few weeks. Darn, wish I'd put a bet on now.'

Skye's stomach did a full forward roll. 'Tell me people are not placing bets on this?'

Julie shrugged. 'You know how the hospital goes. Anyhow, nothing serious, just a box of doughnuts or a round of drinks.' Her hand hit the steering wheel as she sighed. 'It would have been so much better if I'd picked you *both* up.'

Skye sighed and let her tense shoulders release. 'If there wasn't something serious happening, this might have bothered me.'

'Well, it shouldn't. Handsome guy, and not heard anyone say a bad word about him.' She gave Skye a sideways glance. 'You're entitled to some happiness, you know.'

Julie knew all about Skye's mum. Skye gave her a grateful smile. 'I know,' she admitted.

The car pulled into one of the streets around the corner from the hospital and they both jumped out. Skye could see other colleagues pulling up at various spots, all heading in the same direction.

The ambulance bay was empty, and Skye pulled off her jacket before she was even through the door. Two minutes later, her jacket and bag stowed safely in her locker, she reported to the main A&E nurses' station.

'Where do you want me?'

The place was eerily empty. As per the major incident protocol, the patients who had already been in the department had now been decanted to various other places, in preparation for what lay ahead.

Lucas appeared at her side, asking the same question she had. 'Where do you want me?'

The Director of A&E was in place behind the station, his face innately calm. Skye had worked with Ross Colver for years and knew just how good he was. Within a few moments the rest of the staff had assembled and Ross was standing with coloured bibs in his hands for clear identification of roles.

He stood on a chair and addressed them all quickly. 'We've had a major incident called this morning due to a collision of two trains just outside the Fraser Lane stop. Estimates are for around seventy casualties. The Harlington and the Elsborough will share casualties equally. As you can see, our patients are already decanted, and we've sent a team to the site.' He looked at his colleagues. 'Things will get hectic in here, but if you need help, ask for it.' He nodded at Skye. 'Skye and

Lucas will be front door triage.' He handed over red bibs and a pack with coloured triage stickers. 'Allewa will assist.' The experienced admin assistant took the red bib and went to collect a tablet and clipboard.

Ross continued in a steady manner, assigning staff to Resus, Paediatrics, plaster room, cubicles and the waiting area. Skye knew that in all other parts of the hospital—Radiology, labs and some wards, similar decisions would be made. A control room would be set up in the boardroom upstairs to handle the calls, comms and decision-making.

'If you need to eat, drink or pee, do it now,' said Ross as he finished up. 'We're expecting our first ambulance in around ten minutes.'

Skye looked at Lucas. 'I can't think about eating or drinking right now.'

'Me neither.' He grabbed their pack and slipped his bib with *Triage Consultant* over his head.

They headed out to the ambulance bay to take a few minutes before the bedlam began.

'Those poor people,' said Skye as she ran her hands up and down the outside of her arms. 'Catching the train this morning, likely going to work, and thinking it was just going to be another day.'

He slipped his arm around her shoulder. 'If we'd been night shift it's likely we would have been sent out in the primary triage team.'

She shuddered. 'I know. I've done it once before, and is it wrong I'm glad it's not me?'

He shook his head. 'Of course it's not wrong. But equally, I know if you'd been sent you would have done your job just like you should.' He gave her a curious stare. 'Are you sure about the decision you're making—about moving to another job?'

Skye looked out at the dark sky and glowing lights around them. 'You mean will I miss this? Working all the different shifts, and then getting called out in the early hours of the morning?'

He gave an understanding nod. 'I get it.'

'All interviews are in the next few days. And I emailed your GP friend to say thanks for the chat he had with me the other day. It was really useful.'

A distant siren sounded and a fellow colleague with a purple bib appeared. His face was pale. He was one of the paediatricians. 'We might not be able to do all paeds separately,' he warned. 'There were apparently two separate school trips on the trains. There may be too many. I won't be able to assess them all.'

Lucas didn't hesitate. 'Primary or secondary school?'

'Both.'

'You do primary, I'll take secondary,' said Lucas. He gave a nod to Skye and she nodded back in agreement, then turned to Allewa.

'Just get as much info as you can from the kids we triage. Someone at the scene should be co-ordinating where the kids go, but things can get confused, and parents get really upset trying to locate their children.'

Allewa's expression was grave. 'Don't worry, I'll get as much as I can and co-ordinate with the others.'

The blue flashing lights were getting closer and the siren increasing as they approached. Skye took a few breaths. Lucas's warm hand squeezed hers.

'We've got this,' he said with his honest green eyes.

And she believed him. Because she knew he meant it.

Since their kiss they'd spent more time together. They'd gone to the cinema, and for drinks, but still hadn't spent the night together. Skye had previously liked to take things slow in relationships, but she'd never truly felt as comfortable around someone as she did around Lucas. It was the oddest sensation. As if they just fitted together the way they should.

The first ambulance came to a halt and they pulled the doors open. 'Seventy-year-old, impact to chest and head injury, GCS eleven.'

Skye pulled the trolley towards her, with her on one side and Lucas on the other. They worked as a team, assessing the gentleman. His breath sounds on one side were limited, meaning he likely had a collapsed lung. His oxygen levels were adequate whilst he had his mask on, and although his blood pressure was low, it wasn't dangerously so. This man needed treatment and some pain meds but was not in immediate danger.

As they graded him and sent him through, Skye turned to Lucas. 'First time I've not sent a patient with a collapsed lung straight into Resus.'

He reached over and touched her shoulder as they walked to the doors of the next ambulance. 'We only have three Resus beds. He'll get the treatment he needs.'

The doors were already open and their

paed colleague was standing back, as it was clearly a patient for them instead of him.

This time it was a woman. 'Mary Keen, age forty, teacher at Palin Secondary School. She was caught between some seats and has two fractured tib and fibs,' said the paramedic.

Mary's face was so white she was ghost-like and even though Skye could see from her chart she'd been given pain meds, they clearly hadn't had the full effect.

'I need to be back with my class,' she said, wincing as the ambulance trolley moved. 'I don't know how they all are.'

Lucas put his hand over hers. 'Don't worry, our colleagues are there taking good care of them. Let us take care of you.' He assessed her quickly as Allewa took some notes.

The paramedic looked over to the paediatrician. 'There's a few on their way. But most are walking wounded. There are only a few with more serious injuries.' She shook her head and mouthed silently, 'No fatalities that I know of.'

As Lucas graded Mary Keen, Skye could almost feel the relief in the air around them. Her insides had been in knots at the thought of children being on those trains.

Sirens rang in the air again and the first

ambulances moved out of the way to allow others to arrive. It was a steady stream from then on.

Mostly broken bones, and some facial injuries from glass or flying luggage. The majority of the adults were commuters heading into work. A few had been people heading into London to go on to airports, whose trips would now be delayed.

Most of the teenagers had minor injuries. One had their shoulder pinned by a metal part of the window frame of the train and was taken off to Theatre for its safe removal. Another had severe face lacerations from broken glass and was also taken to Theatre by one of the maxillofacial surgeons.

The Harlington was getting busier by the second. Parents, friends and relatives were arriving and, as first suspected, some had been directed to the wrong hospital. Phones were constantly ringing, with workmates trying to find out if their colleagues who hadn't arrived at work had been involved in the accident.

In between all this, the 'normal' ambulances rolled in, since patients hadn't been diverted from the hospital as yet. Pensioners who'd fractured hips on slippery pavements, a young man who'd been stabbed in an early morning mugging and a few people with chest pain, one of whom arrested as soon as the ambulance doors opened.

Police and fire colleagues were also dotted throughout the department, some having attended the scene of the accident and either accompanying patients or having injured themselves. And reporters were everywhere. Most were fine, and followed the instructions from the hospital comms department, but there were always a few rogue reporters, stepping in places they shouldn't or asking questions when they could see people were busy doing their jobs.

All the while, Lucas and Skye were steadily working.

One young girl with a broken arm was part of the *corps de ballet*. She was hysterical as Skye took time to comfort and reassure her. Of course, she wouldn't be able to dance with the cast she would have to wear for the next six weeks. But Skye assured her there would be no reason why she would not be able to continue afterwards. She watched as the young girl was wheeled away in a chair.

'Okay?' asked Lucas at her elbow.

She leaned against him for a few seconds, not really caring who saw. 'Just thinking about her. She's worked so hard to get this place, and this accident could steal that from her.'

'You think?'

'I think that lots of young girls are just waiting for their own chance to make it into the *corps de ballet*. Her worst day is going to be someone else's best.'

She sighed and he slipped an arm around her waist as Ross Colver appeared. If he noticed their position, he didn't mention it.

'You two, coffee and sandwiches in the staffroom. We aren't expecting any more ambulances from the site right now.'

Skye flicked the switch on the machine to give her double the strength of coffee she would normally take. The sandwiches didn't look particularly appetising. Her brain was still in breakfast mode, so she reached for a packet of chocolate digestives instead, settling down next to Lucas on the sofa.

There were a few other people in here that she didn't recognise—likely from other parts of the hospital who had come down to help. She rested her head on his shoulder.

'It's not been too bad,' he said reassuringly, before looking down at a small splatter of blood on his scrubs.

'I can't believe there's no fatalities,' she said wearily. 'It's like a Christmas miracle.'

'I spoke to one of the policemen. They said it was a failure on one of the lines. They were the first trains of the day, and one of the drivers recognised that something wasn't quite right. He'd radioed ahead and both trains had slowed down. It didn't prevent the collision, but things could certainly have been worse.'

She looked up and gave him a smile. 'We worked well together, didn't we?'

'I think so,' he replied, fixing her with those green eyes.

For a few moments it felt as if they were the only people in the room, the others just fading into the background. All she could focus on was the bright green of those eyes, the slight shadow around his jaw line and the slight dark curl of his hair. That, and the way he was totally focused on her.

He was looking at her exactly the way he'd done before they'd shared their first kiss in the linen closet.

'Are you tired?' he asked, his voice barely above a whisper.

She nodded without speaking.

'When we all get stood down, do you want

to come back to mine? You know I'm only a few minutes away from here.'

She knew exactly what he was asking. And she knew exactly what her reply would be. 'Sure, I'd like that.'

His smile widened, and there was a glimmer of something in his eyes. Maybe his face was just reflecting exactly how she felt inside.

'Just think,' she said, 'in three interviews' time, it will be Christmas.'

'Is that how we're counting now?'

'That's how I'm counting,' she said, putting her hand on her chest. 'It's been a long time since I've had an interview. I'm scared I'll blow it.'

'You won't blow it,' he said easily. 'Look at the experience you've got and the skills. You can do bloods, Venflons, IVs, ECGs, set up syringe drivers, dress wounds, diagnose as well as any junior doctor.'

'What about palliative care? There are so many more people choosing to spend their last days at home.' She gulped. 'I only have personal experience of that, or experience where a care package has broken down and someone with end-of-life care ends up in here. GPs and their teams, and district nurses, play a huge role in all that now.'

Her hand was still on her chest, and Lucas put his hand gently over hers. 'And your personal experience is unique. It gives you the knowledge that others might not have, and the perspective of a carer in all this, what they have to take on, and how they can be best supported by the team around them.'

Her eyes flooded with tears. Even when she was having doubts, Lucas could make her feel better, let her recognise her own value in a sea of other potential candidates. The coffee she'd been drinking started to flush through her system, giving her the caffeine kick that her body needed.

'Thank you,' she said, straightening up. 'Ready for the second wave?'

Lucas nodded and they both headed back out into the department. Some parts of the major incident were winding down now. All of the patients from the accident had been taken to the two hospitals. There were still some walking wounded waiting to be seen, but all had minor injuries that would only require some patching up, or a few stitches at most.

The admin staff at The Harlington had kept on top of all patient details, contacting relatives when required, redirecting enquiries and ensuring that all children were accompanied whenever needed. Both schools had also sent extra staff to stay with children whose parents were struggling due to the transport issues the train collision had caused.

Skye set herself alongside another nurse in one of the cubicles and dealt with as many walking wounded as she could. Although the overall number of people injured had been estimated as seventy, the steady stream of walking wounded in The Harlington alone amounted to four hundred.

By the time Skye was pinning her hair up for the umpteenth time, she was truly exhausted.

Lucas appeared around her cubicle a little after six. 'Ross says to go home.' He smiled, and even though she could tell he was just as tired as she was, he still had a sparkle in his eyes.

'What about Ross?' she asked as she pulled her plastic pinny off, deposited it in the bin and washed her hands for the hundredth time.

'What about Ross? If you can persuade that man to go home, then you're a better person than I.'

Skye sighed, realising straight away that

even though Lucas hadn't known Ross as long as she had, he'd certainly got his measure.

She pulled her phone from her pocket. 'Give me five minutes,' she said, disappearing into an office for a moment.

When she came back out, Lucas had his jacket on. 'What were you doing?' he asked as he walked her back to the locker room.

She winked as she grabbed her own jacket and bag. 'Phoning Ross's wife.'

'The big guns?' he joked.

'You know her?' she teased back. 'Biggest heart on the planet, but not to be messed with. She'll persuade him to go home now.'

They walked out, saying goodnight to some fellow colleagues, and Skye felt relieved to finally be getting out of the place.

'Fancy a takeaway?' asked Lucas. 'What about some pizza?'

'Anything,' she said, laying her head against his upper arm. 'I will literally eat anything. And you'd better have some mindless TV for me to watch.'

'Like what?'

'*Friends, Bridgerton, Gilmore Girls, Killing Eve, West Wing, Stranger Things, Star Trek...* Any of the above will do.'

He laughed, 'Oh, I'm sure I'll be able to find you something that will do.'

His phone buzzed and he pulled it out of his pocket and frowned.

'What is it?'

'A message to contact my solicitors as soon as possible.'

Skye stopped walking. 'Is it from Albert?'

Lucas pushed his phone back into his pocket. 'That's what's odd about it. It's from one of those other guys—you remember Mr Bruce?'

She wrinkled her nose. The guy really had been unpleasant and generally quite smug. 'Yeah.' Even the thought of him gave her an uncomfortable feeling.

'Well, he can wait,' said Lucas brusquely.

'What about the other person—the events manager, are you seeing her?'

'Day after tomorrow,' he said, and she could feel him sucking in a big breath. 'And doubtless I'll find out all about the New Year's Eve event.'

Her hand tapped his chest. 'Oh, just as well you'd already offered to work Christmas then, isn't it? You should at least have that night off.'

'I feel as if you're quite amused by this,' he said, a suspicious look in his eyes.

She shrugged and laughed. 'Told you I always prefer New Year. At least we know where the party is, and don't need to hunt one out.'

'How come I instantly feel there's a few stories in there?'

He'd slowed down outside a large glass-fronted apartment block with a concierge at the front door. The dark glass doors slid back without a sound.

'There's more than a few,' she admitted as Lucas nodded at the concierge and led her over to the lifts.

A minute later they arrived on his brightly lit floor and Lucas opened one of four identical dark doors.

He flicked a switch as they walked inside and Skye was struck by how modern and well-maintained the flat was. Somehow, her place on the outskirts just didn't compare.

It was strangely comforting seeing inside his place. The sofas looked comfortable, the kitchen he took her through to had well-stocked cupboards, and as she slid on to one of the comfortable leather stools at the kitchen island, he opened the fridge to offer a variety of drinks.

She shook her head. 'While I'd love a glass of wine, I think I'd just prefer a coffee to go with the pizza. I'm too tired for anything else and it might wake me up a bit.'

He flicked a switch on a nearby machine and stuck in a pod. The coffee was finished just as the pizza arrived and Lucas joined her on a stool at the island as they ate out of the box.

'What do you want to watch?' he asked as they walked through to the living room. The dark windows showed a glittering view of London, and Skye gave a tiny shiver.

'Can people see in?' she asked, looking at the dark towers around them.

Lucas frowned, 'I suppose, in theory, they can. But can you see into anyone else's place right now?'

Even though it seemed voyeuristic, Skye walked up to the window and stared at the surrounding buildings. She could see warm lights, blinds and blurred outlines. A few figures could be glimpsed up close at windows for a fraction of a second. But everyone was too far away for any details. It gave her a little reassurance.

'I just wondered,' she said, rolling her shoulders back to release some of her tension.

'What? That people might see you sitting on the sofa watching *Gilmore Girls*?'

She laughed and nodded. 'Yeah, that. But I'm feeling kind of sci-fi right now.'

He picked up the remote as they settled on the squishy sofa, her fitting comfortably under his arm as he scrolled the TV menu.

'Before you ask—' he sighed '—yes, I did buy a sofa without actually sitting on it. I didn't realise it was quite so soft.'

'It's certainly comfortable,' she joked. 'I might just not be able to get up again.'

'Well, we wouldn't want that,' he said in a low voice.

She turned her head to face him. They hadn't put on any of the main lights, and the only glow was from the TV screen. Her hand moved up and rested on his chest. 'Maybe I don't really want to get up,' she said, her heart beating fast.

He shifted his body so they were face on. 'So, what do you want to do?' he asked, a teasing note in his voice.

She tilted her head to the side. 'There's this man I've been seeing—' she smiled

'—and it's reached a point…' She let her voice tail off.

Lucas picked it up with an equally teasing smile. 'It's reached a point…?'

His hand had moved around to her back, slipping between the gap in her clothes, and his finger was tracing tiny circles on her bare skin.

She tried not to sigh too hard, her brain leaping *way* forward. Instead, she reached up her hand and let her own finger run down his cheek, stopping at his shadowed jaw line where his stubble was rough against her finger pad.

'To see what comes next,' she whispered. Then she made the first move. Pushing him backwards on the sofa so she was above him. It was easy to lie her body on top of his and start kissing him.

In turn, his hand snaked up inside her top again, stroking her skin and toying with her bra strap as he met her kisses with equal passion.

It seemed as if everything had been leading to this. She was exactly where she wanted to be, with the person she wanted to be with.

And all of a sudden, she wasn't so tired any more.

CHAPTER SEVEN

LUCAS WAS AWOKEN by the sound of his buzzing phone. There was a horrible sense of déjà vu as he realised another phone was buzzing too. Skye's. She was snuggled under his arm, her warm bare skin against his. They'd finally made it through to his bedroom, and both were off work today. Their phones shouldn't be buzzing like this.

He gave her a nudge. 'Skye, your phone,' he mumbled, hating the fact that he was going to have to pull his arm out from under hers to detach himself and retrieve his phone from the floor beside them.

She gave a half-hearted mumble, then, at the next buzz, sat bolt upright in bed. The duvet was clutched to her front.

'You've got to be joking,' she groaned as she leapt from the bed, stark naked, and grabbed her phone from the top of the chest of drawers in his room.

He couldn't help but smile at the brief glimpse of her naked form as she grabbed the phone and pulled the covers back over herself.

'Don't,' she said with a raise of her eyebrows.

Her movement gave him the chance to glimpse his own phone and his brow creased in confusion.

'What?'

There was no emergency text from the hospital. Instead, there were multiple missed calls and a few missed texts. A few were from friends, but most were from the solicitors.

Skye was reading the messages on her own phone. Her mouth was open. Her head whipped around.

'What is all this?' she asked.

She held her phone up so he could read the latest message.

Don't read the headlines. Ignore them all.

It was from Ross, their boss.

Lucas picked up his tablet from his bedside table and flicked on the TV at the same time.

The newsreader was reporting on yesterday's train accident. No fatalities. Eighty-six hospital admissions. More than four hundred requiring treatment. An investigation would be taking place over the next few weeks. It was implied that if it had been slightly later in the day, the numbers would have been much worse.

But the newsreader moved onto quite a different subject as the headlines flashed up on his tablet.

The new Duke of Mercia is London's latest billionaire after inheriting the title from his previously unknown father.

Their heads shot up in horror as the newsreader continued to explain a variety of factual information, alongside a whole host of information that seemed more fiction than fact.

Skye leaned over and glimpsed some of the less flattering headlines on his tablet that were currently adorning the red top papers. These were coupled with some slightly unflattering photos, clearly taken last night on their walk home.

Dashing new Duke caught in nurse's snare!

Is it him she loves? Or is it his billions?

The Harlington's hidden doctor is a secret billionaire!

Too late, ladies—the new Duke is already hooked!

Has Cinderella got her hands on the brand-new Duke?

If the headlines weren't bad enough, the reporting that followed was more than a little questionable.

Skye's head was touching his shoulder as he scrolled through the articles. Some described her as plain or unattractive, accompanied by a blurred photo, clearly from Skye's schooldays, showing her wearing her uniform and with her hair pulled back severely in a ponytail. It was like a million other unflattering school photos.

One claimed she was homeless. Another mentioned she lived in the 'poorest part' of London. What on earth would her neighbours in Tower Hamlets make of that?

There was a 'quote' from a colleague: 'Oh, Skye Carter, yes, she'll wrap herself around any doctor that comes along. But this guy? She'll hang on for dear life. She's always been looking for a rich bloke.'

Lucas flinched. He hated all this, and it felt entirely his fault, even though he'd had no knowledge of it.

Skye stiffened next to Lucas, before reaching over and grabbing last night's used scrub top from the floor. She shook her head. 'What on earth is going on? Who has been talking to the press, and how did they find out about you?'

Lucas's phone started to ring, and he thought about ignoring it for a second before he answered. 'Ross,' was his only reply.

This was a nightmare. Not at all what he'd expected. Why on earth was there any interest in who he was dating? His heart clenched in his chest. He'd felt Skye tense next to him, and he didn't blame her. The reporting was ridiculous and hurtful. The last thing he wanted was for Skye to suffer because they'd started dating. At least he assumed they'd started dating. They hadn't even had a chance to have that conversation yet.

He really, really didn't want anything to spoil this. Even before last night, Skye had found a way into his life and his heart in a way he hadn't imagined possible.

Anger was surging through his veins at the thoughtless words and ridiculous headlines. He wanted to protect her. He wanted her to feel safe around him.

Just like he felt around her.

All those thoughts passed through his head in the blink of an eye, and Ross was speaking. So Lucas started to pay attention.

This was a nightmare. She'd woken up to an actual nightmare. She'd heard about other people being attacked in the press before—but she'd never expected it to be her.

All of a sudden, Skye had a wave of understanding and sympathy for the minor celebrities who found themselves under the spotlight, photographed unexpectedly and with every conversation dissected by the press.

It was terrifying. Was this what dating Lucas would mean? It made her blood run cold.

This was new. It was exciting. They'd had a few weeks to get to know each other, and Skye liked every single thing about him. She knew he wasn't perfect—but neither was she.

That was the beauty of getting to know someone. What she didn't want was lies, figments of people's imagination and misinterpretation of facts being printed about her in the press, or online. She had always valued her privacy. The sense of betrayal from some of her colleagues ran deep.

She listened, wondering what Ross might be saying to Lucas. He was a good boss—his text this morning proved that—but her stomach was still in knots.

After a short time Lucas finished the call and looked at Skye.

'What did he say?' she asked.

'He wanted to check that we were both okay...' Lucas started, then he pulled a face. 'And he asked if I was actually a duke.'

'Did you tell him?'

'He's my boss, I could hardly not. Plus—' he sucked in a breath '—it seems like the whole world knows. It's not like I can keep it a secret.' He shook his head and continued. 'So, we both have the next few days off. He asked me to confirm that I would still cover Christmas, and I said yes, obviously.'

A phone sounded, a different kind of ring, and Lucas picked up a regular-looking phone next to his bed. There was a mumbled exchange. He ran his fingers through his hair and replaced the receiver.

'That was the concierge. He said that the building is surrounded by reporters.'

'What?' Skye glanced at the remainder of her crumpled scrubs on the floor. 'Oh, great.'

Lucas sat on the edge of the bed. 'I'm sorry,' he said in a low voice.

'It's not your fault.' She paused for a moment, doing her best to blink back tears. 'But I do wonder how they found out.'

He put an arm around her shoulder and kissed the side of her head. 'So do I,' he sighed. 'I was a fool to think I could keep this quiet. I'm so sorry you've been exposed to all this.'

She stared at the floor for a few seconds. Now was the time. Now was the time to make the decision if she was in or out.

She looked at him, and she could tell he knew exactly what she was thinking.

He brushed her cheek with the softest of touches. 'Not exactly how I dreamed about our first morning together.'

She stared into his green eyes. 'You dreamed about it?' she asked in a quiet voice.

'Of course I did,' he admitted. 'Didn't you?'

And that was it. As the warm feeling

spread across her belly, she knew her decision was made.

'Can my duke take me away from all this?' she asked.

He gave a shaky sigh. She could sense the relief her words had given him, and he squeezed her hand as he stood.

'It's going to be a nightmare to get out of here. Why don't we just take the car? We can go to Costley Hall.'

Skye felt a bit unsure. Her appearance had already been under scrutiny. All she had was the scrubs she'd been wearing the night before. They'd both been so tired there hadn't been a chance to plan ahead. It would be like doing the walk of shame after a hitch-up on a night out.

But no. She shook that thought from her head. There was no walk of shame. This was Lucas, the man she'd grown to know, and to care for deeply. No matter what they said about her, she was going to hold her head high.

'I'll need to get some clothes.'

'No problem. We'll drop by your place on the way.'

Her heart was heavy. This wasn't the way she'd pictured today going. In her head, she'd wanted to wake up in Lucas's arms and have a nice day together. Relaxing, talking about how things might be and looking forward to what might come next.

Her eyes darted to the tablet again. The headlines were ridiculous and mainly untrue. She was just a nurse. No one special. But within a few hours they'd identified her, found old school pictures and apparently found colleagues with dubious opinions of her.

That, undoubtedly, hurt the most.

She'd dated one orthopaedic doctor, four years ago, for around five months. That was the totality of her relationships with doctors at The Harlington. They'd broken up amicably because things hadn't really clicked between them. That was it. Nothing else.

She slipped on her scrub trousers and collected her jacket and bag while Lucas stuffed some things into a rucksack. He grabbed some toiletries, then gave her a nod. 'Ready?'

A few moments later they were in the lift which took them down to the underground garage. The gleaming black Range Rover was parked in one of the spaces.

'Bet you're glad you didn't give that back,' she murmured as they jumped in.

'My other car is still in the garage getting fixed,' he said, 'or else I would have.' He paused for a moment. 'I really should phone and let them know that we're coming, shouldn't I?'

She grimaced, thinking of Donald and Olivia. 'I guess so.' Her insides twisted, wondering if they would be welcome, or at least if *she'd* be welcome, or whether they might actually believe some of the stuff reported in the news today.

Lucas made the call and they pulled out of the underground garage. As he had to pause to pull out onto the main road, a number of photographers spotted them and snapped away. Half an hour later, as they approached her flat, Skye realised there were another few outside her door.

Lucas shot her an anxious glance. 'Do you want to stop, or just continue on?'

She really wanted to go back into her own home, to get some make-up, toiletries, her charger and favourite clothes if they were going to be away for a few days. But the thought of being snapped by more photographers was too much.

'I guess I might be wearing your things for

a day or so. Darn it, I was halfway through a really good book.'

Lucas gave her a half-smile. 'Haven't you heard I'm a billionaire? I can buy you clothes.' He did a swift U-turn on the road and headed in the other direction.

They both started to laugh and Skye felt an unexpected wash of relief. After a stressful day, a wonderful night and a crummy morning, she needed it.

Then something came into her head. 'Oh, no.'

'What?'

They'd stopped at a set of traffic lights.

'I have an interview. Well, three interviews in the next few days.'

'And I've just met my accountant and now have one of those exclusive Coutts cards— like the Queen had.' He shuffled and pulled his wallet from his back pocket, tossing it on to her lap. 'I'm serious. Buy what you need. A suit, some shirts, some shoes. Costley Hall is the billing address and that's where everything will be sent, so just use my name.'

Skye opened his wallet and pulled out the card. She'd never seen one in person. She held it, palm open, and looked at it suspiciously.

'Are you sure?' Then she shook her head and dug around for her own bag.

'Don't you dare,' he growled. 'It's my fault you're in this position, not yours. I've inherited more money than I know what to do with. You know what I've bought so far?'

She shook her head.

'A new sofa,' he joked. 'And you know how those things take months to arrive? I paid so much... It's coming in three days—two days now.'

She wrinkled her nose. 'For your flat?'

He shook his head. 'No, for Costley Hall. I hated the furniture in the main rooms. I ordered a new bed too—it should arrive today, along with new bedding.' He gave a hollow laugh. 'None of it will be in keeping with the rest of the furnishings, but I figured at least one part of Costley Hall I can decorate myself.'

The words made her skin tingle a little. 'So, you're getting used to the idea?' she asked tentatively.

'I'm buying some time,' he said, and then groaned as he obviously realised how literal those words were. 'I've spoken to the events planner, Brianna, but haven't met her yet. She seems nice. And actually quite fierce. And since I don't have a pre-booked holiday on New Year's Eve, I can't really get out of the ball.' He gave her a sideways glance. 'And I'm kind of hoping that neither can you.'

She gave him a little smile as a warm glow spread through her. 'You're asking me on a date?'

'I'm asking you to be my partner in crime.' He smiled, then paused. 'Yes, I'm asking you on a date.'

She didn't say the words that were currently circling in her head. That sad thought that still kept bubbling up when she least wanted it to. It was nearly Christmas and New Year. This would be her first without her mum. Her first alone.

It actually hurt much more than she'd expected it to. Of course she'd known it would be difficult. But she hadn't realised it was the little things that would catch her unawares. Catching sight of an advert for a TV programme they'd always watched together at Christmas. Pulling out the Christmas decorations and gently touching the ones that her mother had bought for her once she'd got her own place. Unpacking her winter clothes and finding the pink and purple bobble hat that her mother had got her the year before, and the giant bed socks with pom-poms down the front because her feet were always freezing at night. Finishing the last of the lemon marmalade that her mother had always bought especially for her, from goodness knew where, because none of the supermarkets seemed to stock it these days.

Being somewhere different—somewhere new—at New Year's Eve would be a blessing. Being there with Lucas might be something else entirely.

It was almost as if Lucas was reading her thoughts, sensing her mood right now.

'Ever wanted to do something completely mad? Throw all caution to the wind? Well, that's what I want you to do for the next hour. Order everything that you want. Your makeup. Your perfume—everything you would have brought from home and couldn't collect. All you need for your interviews. A new laptop. And a ballgown, because you'll need one. The book you were half reading. Order it all. And then order more.'

He was lifting his hands from the steering wheel now, throwing them outwards in enthusiasm.

She laughed at him. 'It's a wonderful idea, but I'm not sure I'm designed that way.'

'Order the parrot chair!' he shouted, and she jumped in her seat. 'Order the chaise longue too!'

Her skin tingled at the thought. How to go wild? To just spend money without worrying? Skye had never been in that position. Living in London made that impossible, except for the very rich. She had a budget she stuck to. She always made sure her bills were paid and her rent was covered. She saved if she wanted something. She wasn't poor, but she didn't have thousands stashed in the bank either. Her mother had taken out life insurance nine years before she'd died and whilst she was still in good health, so Skye knew that eventually, when everything was settled, she might have a little inheritance, but that was it. No golden goose. No big nest egg.

'Go on, Skye, why not? I probably earn more in interest than some people get paid. I haven't decided what to do with the money yet. But I can guarantee you that anything you spend in the next hour won't even scratch the surface.'

He was holding this imaginary gift in front of her, dangling it, where she could reach out and touch it.

'I don't have anywhere to put a chaise longue,' she said simply.

'Then pick a room at Costley Hall,' he said. 'It will brighten the place up. Go for it.'

Her mouth opened, and then closed again. She did need some make-up and clothes for the next few days. This could be fun. Even if she only did it for five minutes. She gulped. 'I'll get some essentials.'

As they continued through the London streets, Lucas started playing some music. Skye bought her usual make-up, underwear, one pair of jeans, a jacket, four tops and a pair of pyjamas—though she wasn't entirely sure she would need those. All from the regular high street stores where she usually shopped. Then she took a breath and ordered a black suit jacket and skirt, a pair of black court shoes and a bright pink and identical red shirt for her interviews.

These things were slightly different. They weren't identical to what she had at home. She'd planned to buy some new shirts, to wear alongside a slightly tired suit she had from a few years ago. Again, she bought from a high street store she favoured, rather than any of the fancy or exclusive boutiques in London. She paid for everything with Lucas's

card, even though her fingers were a bit hes-
itant, then slid the card back into his wallet
and put her phone back in her lap.

She glanced up. They were heading out
of London now. Thirty minutes had literally
passed in a blur.

'Did you get the parrot chairs?'

She shook her head. 'Just some replace-
ment clothes. And some things for my interviews. Thank you for that. I appreciate it.'

'What about a ballgown? Did you get one
of those?'

She started to laugh. 'No, I didn't get a
ballgown. I didn't even look. Let's worry
about that later.'

He shot her a pretend serious glance. 'But
if I talk you into a ballgown, then you can't
really duck out of the ball. Don't you see my
cunning plan here?'

She leaned back against the soft leather of
the car seat and took a deep breath. Everything was moving at a million miles an hour.
And even though the headlines hadn't been
flattering about her, she was starting to push
that to the back of her mind.

Lucas was here. He was by her side. And
after last night she was even more sure that
this was where she wanted to be. But maybe

once he realised how much being a duke actually meant, he might look for a girlfriend who had the same social standing. The thought gave her uncomfortable feelings and, for the first time ever, she was glad her mum wasn't around to see those headlines. On any other day she would have absolutely loved for her mum to have the chance to have met Lucas, but that just wasn't to be, and she had to accept that.

She glanced upwards just as they started to reach the outskirts and the area around them became greener. The pale blue sky made her wonder if her mum was up there, and what she might be thinking. Would she be happy for Skye? Or think she was completely out of her depth?

Lucas's phone started to ring again, this time coming through the console on the car. He pressed the accept button and, unfortunately, Mr Bruce's nasal tones came through the speaker.

'Your Grace, we need to have a discussion about your colleague, the young lady, Skye Carter.'

Skye immediately stiffened, all her senses on alert.

'We don't,' said Lucas in a voice she'd only

heard a few times. 'I'm not interested in what you have to say about Skye—unless it's a way to stop the false reporting.'

Mr Bruce cleared his throat. It should have been a completely innocent sound but, for some reason, it had the same smugness and know-it-all manner as everything else he did. He was going to speak again.

Lucas ended the call.

Skye blinked as her eyes filled with tears she was determined not to shed. What on earth were these people going to say about her? There really was nothing to say.

Her heart plummeted. 'What if my potential new employers see the news and think I'm not a good nurse?'

Lucas bristled next to her. She knew this wasn't his fault. He hadn't asked for any of this. But neither had she.

Her thoughts were swirling. Did she have regrets about moving their relationship further on last night? No. But would she have got into a relationship with Lucas in the first place if she'd known there was going to be this kind of fallout? The truth was, maybe not. And that made her uncomfortable.

Because she liked him. She liked him a lot.

Skye wasn't the kind of girl who liked to be

the centre of attention. No one would describe her as a wallflower, but she would never choose to be on the front page of a newspaper.

'I'm sure it will be fine,' said Lucas, but his voice didn't sound quite so convincing.

She sat back into the seat again and tried to think about something else. They had a few days, then it would be Christmas, then it would be New Year. She had no idea what might be involved in the New Year's ball, but Lucas was obviously starting to take his role seriously. He'd met with the accountant. And spoken with the events planner.

As the winding country roads passed by in a welcome flash of white, brown and sometimes green, it seemed as if the countryside had developed into a scene from a Christmas card with snow covering as far as the eye could see.

As they reached Costley Hall, Lucas drew the car to a sudden halt. The huge metal gates were closed, and a number of individuals were skulking around outside. Reporters. Again.

'Must be a slow news day,' he muttered, before phoning the Hall and asking Donald about the gates. The reporters and photographers were around the car quickly, shouting questions through the windows.

A few moments later, the gates slid back and Lucas headed up the driveway, nearly catching a particularly obnoxious reporter with the wing mirror of the car. None of the photographers were stupid enough to be stuck on the wrong side of the gates as they closed again.

Skye let out her breath. 'Is it always going to be like this?'

'Of course not. By tomorrow, I'll be old news. You know what they say about today's news being tomorrow's chip paper.'

She waited until they pulled up at the main door and jumped out, looking down at her scrubs again and wishing she had her own clothes. Lucas grabbed his bag and they walked to the main door. This time, Lucas didn't knock, he just pushed it open and went inside.

Olivia appeared quickly. 'There you are. Those frightful people have been there since this morning. Are you two okay?' She blinked and couldn't hide the fact she looked Skye up and down. It nearly made Skye want to burst into tears.

But it was almost as if Olivia caught that feeling.

'I couldn't get back to my own place to get my things,' Skye explained, trying not to let her voice shake. 'They were outside my flat too. I've been wearing these scrubs since yesterday.'

Olivia walked over and touched her arm. 'Can I make you some tea? Run you a bath?'

Skye had never been good at accepting help, but on this occasion she nodded.

'Come on up to the Duke's suite,' she said. 'I'll start the bath for you, then bring you up some tea.'

'Thank you,' Lucas interjected. 'And our other guest?'

Skye had turned towards the stairs and she looked over her shoulder. 'What other guest?'

Olivia and Lucas exchanged a glance.

'Albert Cunningham has moved in. Well, he's not really, because he's stayed here before. But the hospital wouldn't discharge him without some adaptations in his house. He would have ended up still in at Christmas, so I suggested he come here, where we have some rooms specially adapted while he waited.'

His words made her heart swell.

'Albert's fine,' said Olivia, and Skye could tell she was talking about an old friend. There was a familiarity in her tone. 'The room has everything he needs, and he's using the lift to get up and down. I think he's actually in the library right now.'

'You never told me about Albert,' Skye said, looking at him curiously.

'It was meant to be a surprise, but things just got away from me this morning.'

She nodded, then came back and reached for Lucas's bag. 'I'll need to steal something of yours to put on before I come back down and meet him.'

Lucas gave a nod. 'We've ordered quite a few parcels that will arrive probably later today and tomorrow.'

If Olivia was surprised, she didn't show it. 'I'll let Donald know,' she added simply, then followed Skye up the stairs.

It was nice to be fussed over for once. Olivia found some rose and jasmine bubble bath, and a large dressing gown for Skye. The bath was ready surprisingly quickly and, by the time she came back out, there was a pot of tea and some scones waiting for her.

She looked around the room and smiled,

thinking of the parrot chair and chaise longue and wondering what Olivia would make of them.

Then that deep down feeling surged up again. The one that had been echoed in the news headlines. Was she really good enough to be here? To fit into this grand lifestyle? Her whole London rental could fit into this giant room alone, and that thought made her swallow, her mouth instantly dry.

She walked over to the window and looked over the well-kept beautiful grounds. She was jumping a million miles ahead here. But she knew how she felt about Lucas. She hadn't told him yet, because she was too nervous.

But what if he was having the same thoughts she was? They'd met before either of them had known about his title or estate. What if Lucas was now taking time to contemplate what the future might mean for him, and there wasn't a place in it for Skye?

She sucked in a breath and blinked back tears. That was the trouble with overthinking things, anticipating the worst instead of the best. Their relationship had evolved over weeks, taking the next step when both were ready. He'd been supportive to her, and understanding. And just being in his company made her world feel right.

It was time to stop being paranoid and get back to reality. Get back to how being with Lucas made her feel. She walked back over to the table and sat down.

Lucas appeared at the door. 'Knock, knock.' She instantly smiled, the warm feeling spreading across her body.

He came in and joined her at the table, stealing one of the scones. 'Hey—' she gave his hand a light slap '—get your own!'

He pulled a face. 'I've actually just had one downstairs. But the company up here was too tempting.'

Her smile widened ever further. 'I've just thought of something,' she said.

She looked around the room again. 'Olivia called this place the Duke's suite. She means you—not your father.'

Lucas sat back for a few seconds, as if he was trying to compute what she'd just said. 'My father used the other rooms.' He nodded. 'And it just didn't feel right going in them. She asked me when I spoke to her the other day if I wanted her to prepare rooms for me.'

Skye leaned forward, and she had a teasing glint in her eye. 'Did you warn her about the parrot chair?'

Lucas choked on his scone. When he finally stopped coughing and took a sip of tea, he looked at her. 'I wondered if they might be better in the library. You already declared that your favourite room.'

His green eyes were fixed on hers. She had the weirdest feeling. The kind she'd had as a child, when she tasted sherbet for the first time and it gave her that fizzy sensation, not just on her tongue but all over her body. She nearly didn't say the words that were in her head, but then she just couldn't help it.

'Am I allowed to have a favourite room here?'

She could swear the air crackled around them.

Lucas didn't answer straight away. He just stood up and leaned across the table, his lips connecting with hers.

It wasn't a sweet and tender kiss, nor a madly passionate one. It was solid, safe and reassuring. It gave the message of belonging and for the first time since her mother had died Skye had a feeling of connection and family again.

As his lips parted from hers, he stayed with his face just a few inches from hers.

'You can pick all the rooms you like, and fill this whole place with parrot chairs as far as I'm concerned,' he breathed. 'Just as long as you stay.'

And her world got even brighter.

CHAPTER EIGHT

IT HAD BEEN three days of bliss. Skye was still
in awe of Costley Hall. She'd found a cinema
and a snooker room, alongside the biggest
ballroom that seemed fitting for Cinderella.

Brianna, the event co-ordinator, was scary,
but in a good way. Skye admired her organ-
isational skills, attention to detail and passion for her job. Or, more, her passion for the
charities she was determined to support. The
best laugh was the fact that Lucas seemed in
awe of her too and had gone along with most
of her plans.

Skye had watched the transformation of
the ballroom, from its glittering chandeliers
being lowered and cleaned, to the wooden
floor being highly polished and the gold and
silver decorations being tastefully placed
around the room. Brianna supervised all of

this with an eternal smile on her face and an endless supply of energy.

In amongst all this, Skye attended three separate interviews. Two with the different GP practices and the third with the trust sponsoring the district nurse training places. The black suit fitted perfectly, as did the shoes, and she'd answered all the questions without any problems. All the interviewers had been completely professional, and no one had made any mention of any of the news stories.

She still wasn't sure of where she wanted to be work-wise, and that made her distinctly uncomfortable. When she'd trained as a nurse and had a placement in A&E, she'd known immediately it was for her. She'd thought that having these interviews might have given her the same sense of belonging and an excitement and urgency for a new role. But that hadn't happened. Yet…

She was just crossing back through the ballroom when Olivia found her. 'Another parcel has arrived. It seems to be books. Donald has put them through in the library for you.'

Skye smiled. The books that she'd ordered wouldn't possibly fit with the much more impressive tomes that were currently in there, but there might be a corner she could find for them.

'I'm feeling a bit like Cinderella with all these parcels arriving,' she admitted, and she wasn't joking. Whilst she knew everything that she'd ordered in the car on the way here, it seemed that Lucas had ordered a bit more for her too. That was the danger of using his card. Now he knew her preferences and sizes, and had added some fun stuff too. Parcel after parcel had arrived, and it was ridiculous how much joy she'd felt in the last few days.

Maybe it was just being away from everything. Costley Hall, while ancient, was still like a little piece of paradise, a different world. Skye had never been in a position where she could just order anything she wanted, and she'd curtailed herself even though Lucas had encouraged her. It just didn't seem right when she came across so many patients where poverty and inequalities were a real factor in their lives. So, her half-hour spending spree in the car had come to an end. These books were the last part.

She still wondered if she really fitted in such a grand place. Lucas hadn't said a single thing to make her feel like that, but inside she still feared she might not be able to live up to what would be expected of anyone who was his girlfriend.

As she approached the library there was a distinctive smell of coffee and the sound of hearty laughter. As she peered around the corner, she saw Albert and Lucas sitting in the high-backed red leather Chesterfield chairs, a box of books perched on a table between them.

Skye put her hand on her hip. 'Are you guys laughing at my book choices?' she said.

Both heads turned towards her and she noticed that Albert already had an open book in his lap.

Lucas lifted his coffee mug and took another sip. 'Albert said they are the only decent books in here for years. He's already claimed one as his own.'

Skye moved into the library and pulled over another chair to join them. 'How are you feeling, you book thief?' she asked Albert.

'Good,' he said, holding up the crime thriller he'd picked. 'But don't plan on hiding any of the others away. I'll read them all.'

Skye laughed out loud as she reached into the box and picked out a pile to stack on one of the nearby shelves. She'd ordered a selection of reading material, some old favourites, others new releases. As she put them on the shelves, she shook her head.

'Okay, we have some more thrillers, some sci-fi, a few non-fiction, a couple of older children's books, some women's fiction, some romance and...' she waved a few floppy books in the air '...these ones are a bit racy—you've been warned,' she said as she stuck them on the shelf.

'Young people,' pooh-poohed Albert. 'You think you invented racy.'

Lucas started to laugh again. Albert relaxed into his chair and looked over at Lucas. 'This would have meant everything to your father—to see you here like this.'

Lucas shifted a little, and Skye knew he was still a bit uncomfortable about all this.

'Have you heard from your mother yet?' asked Albert.

It was a loaded question. They all knew it.

'She's still avoiding me,' Lucas admitted. 'I've asked her numerous questions and she keeps refusing to answer them—or not refusing exactly, just saying she'll let me know... eventually.'

Albert raised his eyebrows and sighed. 'Did you do what I suggested?'

Skye sat back down next to them both. 'Okay, so I'm intrigued. What?'

Albert sighed. 'I told Lucas she'd appear in a heartbeat if her allowance is stopped.'

Lucas glanced at Skye. 'I stopped her payments last week.'

Skye was surprised. 'But wasn't something about that included in the will?' she asked.

'It was,' sighed Albert. 'Ginny had a rock-solid legal agreement with Lucas's father. He couldn't have it stopped. But…' he glanced at Lucas '… Lucas didn't. It might be included as a condition in the will, but I doubt it's enforceable.' He shrugged his shoulders. 'There is another idea, which I didn't like to suggest before now.' There was mischief in his eyes.

'What?' Lucas asked cautiously.

Albert gave a rueful smile. 'You tell her I'm here.'

'What will she do?' Skye asked.

'Probably arrive like a bat out of hell.'

Skye sat back. Albert was a nice and perfectly reasonable man. She couldn't quite understand why Ginny—a woman she hadn't even met—would react in that way.

Albert looked tired. 'I wonder what kind of life you might have lived,' he said as he looked at Lucas, 'if we hadn't lived in such a time of prejudice.'

Skye's skin prickled. Now, she understood.

And it was as if someone had pushed Albert's buttons. 'Your father was in his early forties during the eighties. He lost a very good friend to HIV and, like the rest of the world, he was scared. He got married, tried to settle down and have a family, but Ginny very quickly realised that he didn't love her the way she wanted him to.' He gave a sad sigh. 'She took her opportunity to blackmail him and threatened to expose him to all his older family and friends.' He looked at them both. 'These days, it wouldn't have mattered, and wouldn't have worked. But there was still a lot of prejudice in the eighties. The newspapers would have loved a scoop about the Duke not being conventional and the chance to "out" him. So, he went with what Ginny wanted, even though it meant a risk.'

'A risk?' Lucas's voice was a little hoarse and she knew instantly that he was finding this very emotional.

'Yes,' Albert clarified. 'Ginny implied that there would still be contact between the Duke and you, but she wouldn't agree to it in writing. Demanded full custody. As soon as the papers were signed and she had her money, she vanished in a puff of a smoke, and you with her.'

Albert shook his head. 'You have no idea how hard he tried to find you. He always hoped when you turned eighteen you would get in touch. He had no idea what your mother had told you.' His expression was grave. 'He would have been horrified that you didn't even know of his existence, or who you were.'

Skye was struggling to really understand. She'd always known who her parents were. Her father had died from a heart attack five years ago, which had only made her bond with her mother even stronger. She couldn't imagine having half of her life, or her story, missing, even though she knew lots of people who had lives like that.

'That's terrible. I can't believe she'd do something like that. How could she?'

There was a flash of something in Lucas's eyes. 'Maybe other things were going on that none of us know about.'

Skye was surprised. He hadn't ever said anything particularly affectionate about his mother before. He'd been quite frank about what he thought about her lack of contact. But it was clear that deep down there was still an element of denial there. His mother was the only parent he'd ever known; of course he would have loyalty to her.

Still, the stopping of the payments surprised her. Did it mean that Lucas actually just wanted to see his mother, and this was his way of getting her attention—rather than it actually being about the money?

But, before she could think any further, Lucas reached out and took her hand, obviously surprised by his own snappiness. 'Sorry,' he said in a low voice.

She was a little startled, but that small act of taking her hand seemed to relax him a bit, and she watched as the tension in his shoulders eased and he looked back to Albert with a sincere gaze.

'Albert, tell me more about my dad.'

For a moment Albert said nothing. It was the dad word. The more affectionate term than 'father' that had been banded around a few times. It was the first time Skye had heard Lucas say it. She gave his hand a squeeze back, and settled into her chair to listen.

CHAPTER NINE

THEY WERE IN the kitchen, quietly making tea together. Lucas knew that he'd snapped, but Skye seemed to have accepted his apology. The stories Albert had told them had filled him with melancholy about the life he'd missed out on.

And it wasn't about this place. It wasn't about Costley Hall. Or maybe it was, just a little. It was more about the man. Albert—who accepted he might have a skewed point of view—had described a warm, intelligent, bright man, who might occasionally have been slightly outrageous and enjoyed a good party.

Lucas was trying to get his head around what life might have been like if he'd got to stay in one place, make more friends and spend time with his father. He knew that the glimmer of anger and resentment in him was probably entirely normal, so it was hard for him to understand his earlier reaction when Skye had said something about his mother. He'd been the first to tell Skye she hadn't been around much, or kept in touch, and their relationship was certainly fractured. But he felt as if he could say all these things. So why was it different when it came from someone else's mouth?

A hand brushed his jacket sleeve and he turned around. It was Brianna and her face was flushed.

'Someone is causing a scene. She's along in your suite. Says she's your mother.'

Lucas's heart dropped like a stone. His mother. Of course.

Skye was clearly surprised. 'Lucas?' she asked.

He slipped his hand into hers. 'Time to meet my mother, I guess,' he said in a grim tone as they started down the corridor and up the curved staircase.

Anger thrummed through him. Her answers to his emails had been curt, phone and text messages simply ignored. He had a suspicion of why she was here. And he would actually hate for it to be confirmed.

They entered his suite to see his mother

tossing clothes to the floor. *Skye's* clothes. Toiletries and cosmetics had been flung from the bathroom across the floor. His mother was standing amongst all this mess with a look of fury on her slightly too sun-kissed face, which would have highlighted her wrinkles if they hadn't been Botoxed into non-existence.

'This is my room,' his mother hissed as he made his way into the suite.

It had been five years since he'd seen his mother in the flesh. She was still wearing the same perfume, which hung in the air between them. But the familiar scent brought no fond memories. Just a host of disappointment and bitterness. She was dressed in a bright orange coat and fur hat, looking as if she were about to attend a royal event.

He looked at the mess on the carpet, all Skye's belongings.

'This is my suite,' he said in a low voice. 'And I'd thank you to stop destroying what isn't yours.'

There were two designer suitcases in the room, alongside a huge trunk.

'This isn't your room.'

'It is.' He kept his voice icily cold. He'd dealt with his mother's rages before, but he'd never really understood her hidden resentment or her odd behaviour. 'It's mine, and Skye's.'

'Her?' His mother's voice was incredulous. 'This little money-grabber? What do you actually know about her? Oh, wasn't it convenient that she was around to help you with your new discoveries? Anyone would think she'd planned it.'

Lucas nearly choked. 'Don't be so ridiculous. How could you even think that?'

His mother pointed across the room at Skye. 'Because I looked her up. Of course I did. You became an instant billionaire. Of course she would latch on to you.'

He turned to look at Skye, mainly to reassure her that he knew this was absolute nonsense. But something stopped him. Skye looked shell-shocked. She was staring at his mother in the most curious way. In short, she was horrified.

His mother continued. 'I know her,' she spat. 'She was a nurse at one of the clinics I went to in Harley Street. Who knows what I said under anaesthetic, but she was clearly clever enough to track you down before the lawyers did.'

Skye blinked. Her hands were clasped in

front of her and her arms were trembling. She shook her head and glanced at Lucas.

'Skye?' he asked. He wasn't asking about his mother's accusations. He was asking about the look on Skye's face.

Skye lifted one hand to her face. It was almost as if she was trying to force herself to speak.

His mother kept talking at the top of her voice, twittering on and on about how it was all a conspiracy, and Skye was trying to steal his money, or *her* money.

Lucas lifted his hand and put it on Skye's shoulder. He'd never seen her silent like this before. She was feisty and definitely able to stand up for herself. She'd never let someone treat her like this in A&E.

Unless, of course…no. No, he wasn't even going to go there.

'Skye,' he said quietly, 'are you okay?'

She blinked and stared up at him. 'I do know your mother,' she said in a stiff voice.

He glanced back over his shoulder.

'See!' shouted his mother in glee. 'She looked you up, and saw we were connected. She realised the Duke was dead and that you would inherit everything. She planned this all along. She targeted you from the moment you started at The Harlington.'

There was a flash in his peripheral vision and he realised Albert had entered the room.

It was almost as if there was now another target for his mother. She turned all her attention from Skye onto Albert, treating him with equal venom.

'You're still here! Shouldn't you be dead by now? Haven't you bled this family dry already?'

Albert seemed completely unperturbed by this orange vision with the highest pitched voice Lucas had ever experienced. He sighed. 'Genevieve, a delight to see you, as always.' He gave a gentle shrug of his shoulders. 'Or maybe not,' he added simply.

Lucas felt as if he were in some kind of reality TV show. His mother had always been highly strung and self-centred, but he'd never seen a display like he was currently witnessing. But it was apparent that Albert had seen this kind of behaviour before and couldn't have cared less. He gave a worried glance towards Skye, moved across the room and positioned himself on the parrot chaise longue.

Lucas realised what he was doing. He was deliberately making himself the target. He must have heard Genevieve screeching at Skye and decided to intervene.

Lucas held up his hand again. 'Enough!' This time he shouted, gaining his mother's full attention.

He pointed at her. 'Don't you dare come into my home and act like this. You won't answer my calls or emails. You've lied to me for the entirety of my life, and now you think you can appear and make ridiculous claims against the woman I love? Well, no. I won't stand for it. I don't know where you came from, but you can just head on back there.' Rage was flooding his veins, pent-up feelings from years of being virtually ignored by his mother.

He turned back to Skye. Her face was the palest he'd ever seen it.

'I looked after her post-operatively,' she said quietly. 'I do remember her—' she took a breath '—but I didn't look into anything about her, and I had no idea you were her son.'

It took him a few moments to realise what she was saying.

'Skye,' he said, looking into her eyes in confusion. 'I don't believe a single word she says. I don't think for a second you knew we were connected. I don't believe that you knew I was a duke before I did. Don't listen to her, don't listen for a moment.'

He turned back to his mother, who was ranting again at Albert.

He moved across the room quickly. 'You've had years,' he said coldly. 'Years to tell me about all of this. Yes, I get that you were hurt. I get that my father's interests lay elsewhere. But you don't get to come here and speak to my family like that.'

'Family?' she yelled back indignantly. 'I'm your family.'

'Really?' His voice was dangerously low. 'Then when are you going to start acting like it? I had a father. A father you told me was dead. And now he is. And guess what? I don't remember meeting him. You stole a lifetime of memories from me because you were slighted. A lifetime of chances to get to know him. And now I have a wonderful girl-friend. And you seem determined to alienate her too. And Albert—who I understand you might have history with, but who I happen to like, and he can help me fill in the gaps about my father too. So, if you don't understand how I feel about all this, you can leave. And stop living off my father's wealth.'

The elephant in the room had been addressed and there was silence. Genevieve's mouth was open as if she was just about to start again, but had been stopped mid flow. Her face was red, clashing horribly with her orange coat, which she still wore. Albert's eyes were fixed on the floor. He'd done what he'd set out to, and taken the focus off Skye.

'Let's face it, you're not here because you love me, or are worried about me. You're here because I cut off your monthly allowance.'

'It's my money,' his mother shouted, 'not yours!'

Something washed over Lucas. Almost as if Albert had whispered in his ear. Or maybe it was his father?

There was no point fighting with this woman. No point arguing.

'Apparently not,' he said in a low voice. 'So, just leave.'

There was a gasp behind him. Lucas spun round. Skye had a single tear rolling down her cheek.

'You can't ask her to leave,' she said, as if something was caught in her throat.

'Of course, I can. She's spent most of my life absent anyway. I don't need her. I don't want her.'

'Don't say that,' choked Skye. 'You can't say that.'

He was still so angry with his mother that he couldn't take a moment to understand the pain that Skye had in her eyes.

She stepped forward so that only he could hear her speak. 'This is too much,' she whispered, her eyes wide and her voice croaky. Her hand reached up to his cheek. 'The man I love wouldn't do that. He wouldn't tell his mother to leave and cut her off. Stop, Lucas. Think for a minute. I don't have my mother any more, and I would do anything—*anything*—to have her back. You can fix this. You can repair this relationship with your mother. You've both been hurt, but it's time. It's time to sit down and fix this. You have to. Because I don't see a future for us otherwise.'

'What?' He couldn't believe his ears. 'Did you hear what she said about you? What she thinks of you? I'm defending you, and I will always put you first, Skye. Always.'

More tears flowed and her hand lowered from his cheek. 'She doesn't know me, Lucas. She doesn't know me at all. But she does know you. You're her only son. The most important human being on the planet to her. You have to work at this. Families are hard, Lucas.

People don't just grow up in a happy bubble. All families take work. I need to know that you're prepared to work at this, just like you'll be prepared to work at us over the years.'

He looked over his shoulder. His mother was still standing there, stiffly, defiantly, with a hostile look in her eyes. He knew that she would spend her life trying to get between him and Skye. And he couldn't tolerate that. Not for a moment.

He turned back to Skye, but she was gone. Gone from the room. It was as if she already knew what he was going to tell her, and she hadn't waited to find out. Because she knew him. She knew him better than he knew himself.

And she'd already decided she couldn't live like that.

CHAPTER TEN

IT WAS OFFICIALLY the worst Christmas ever.

Things would have been much better if A&E had been crammed with patients. Instead, it was as if the whole world had decided to behave on this day. As she walked into the department, she could almost hear the quietness echo around her.

Being on duty with Lucas today would be torture.

Skye had borrowed the least expensive car in the garage and driven home. Donald hadn't even questioned her tear-stained face, just handed over the keys, explained a few things and put a hand on her shoulder, telling her to drive carefully.

Lucas had phoned and texted but she hadn't answered. She needed time. She needed space.

His mother had been a whirlwind of horror.

Exactly the kind of person anyone wouldn't want in their life. Skye certainly didn't want her in her own life.

But she knew better than to say that.

Families were complicated. All the words Genevieve had said had echoed all the fears that Skye already had in her own head. It was bad enough reading them online, but having someone say them to her face…?

Deep down, she had the worst feeling. It didn't matter how Genevieve had behaved towards her. Well, it did. But Skye had been long enough on this earth to know she had to step back and try and get some perspective.

In one way, she was delighted about the fact that Lucas had stood up for her and told his mother to leave.

But ultimately? It would be destructive and selfish.

If Lucas couldn't see her perspective right now—and she got that—because of how all this had been dumped on him from a great height—it was her job to try and make him see it.

The last thing she wanted to be was the reason that Lucas cut off his last remaining parent. No matter how horrid the woman was.

Skye's mother had been warm-hearted and

considerate—traits Skye wasn't sure that Genevieve possessed. But it didn't matter, because she was still Lucas's mother. And after losing her own mum she was left with that deep down regret of not having another hug or another conversation.

Skye believed that someone would only know how that felt if they'd walked in her shoes. She didn't want Lucas to have regrets—for them to stay together and then, when Genevieve eventually died, for him to have resentment or regret that he hadn't worked things out with her.

If she and Lucas stayed together, she knew, ultimately, that could mean having to tolerate someone in her life who would be difficult, likely interfering and mean at times. But Skye was confident that they would be able to work something out, to lay ground rules, to keep things cordial.

She gulped as she glanced over a set of patient notes. Because, deep down, she was considering something else. If Lucas didn't want to take the time and trouble to attempt to sort things out with his mother, would he want to take the time and trouble to sort things out between them, if they ran into trouble further down the road in their relationship? Or would he just walk away and cut her off, like he'd threatened his mother?

It was a horrible, scary prospect. But one she had to consider.

In between all this, she still had to decide what to do about her career. All three jobs had been offered to her, and she needed to make a decision quickly. Did she want to be a practice nurse or a district nurse? Did she want to stay in London or move to the outskirts and nearer the country? And how, when all this was going on, could she even consider something as silly as Christmas?

Bryn, one of her colleagues, settled into the seat next to her as others gathered around for the handover, which was brief and precise.

Her colleagues greeted the day shift with enthusiasm, mainly because their night shift was now finished and they'd be going home to their families. The department was littered with Christmas chocolates. There were only a few patients in the department so far. A miserable baby with a high temperature, two elderly and confused patients who both had infections, a young homeless man who'd been found freezing in a doorway and was suffering from hypothermia, and a middle-aged woman with chest pain.

Lucas was hovering near the back, staying out of Skye's line of sight. Maybe he didn't want to talk to her. Maybe he'd decided to draw a line under their relationship because she hadn't responded to his texts or messages.

Maybe it had been a wrong decision. Because now, and for the next twelve hours, they were going to have to spend the whole shift tiptoeing around each other, under the watching eyes of their colleagues, who were bound to notice that something was off between them.

It wasn't the first time that Skye wished she could pick up the phone to her mum. She would know what to say about all this. She would know what to say to make Skye feel better.

Christmas might not be her favourite time of year, but Skye took a shaky breath and blinked back tears. What she wouldn't do right now for a giant hug…

There were a few comments. A few jokes about whether he still had time to come to work, or was he too busy counting his money. The truth was, Lucas had expected to be ribbed by his work colleagues. He didn't want people to tiptoe around him. He was more worried about what they might be saying about Skye. The news reports had bothered him—not because he'd believed them, but more because he could see how hurt she'd been by some of the comments from unknown colleagues—even though she'd tried to hide it.

Lucas knew that some of it might just be made up—anything for a headline or a story—but if he caught anyone saying something untoward about Skye he wouldn't hold his tongue for a second.

The last few days at Costley Hall had been awful. All because of his mother.

Up until that point, it had almost felt as if things were clicking into place.

He couldn't pretend to know even half of what was going on at the estate, but he was learning and that was the important thing. He'd made some headway with Brianna, the events co-ordinator, and hoped they could be on the same wavelength. He'd met all the stable staff and gardeners. He enjoyed Albert's company. No one had come out and said it yet, but he knew that Albert had been his father's partner and had lived at Costley Hall, in one way or another, for over twenty years.

But most of all he'd loved being around

Skye. She was warm, friendly and always looking to help in any way she could. Olivia and Donald liked her, and she'd asked about things he hadn't even thought of—such as whether Costley Hall bought their produce from local vendors and supported the nearby village in any way.

He'd spent most days with her constantly in his line of sight. He couldn't help but look at her. Her laughter had filled the air at times. He'd also caught her in a few quiet moments when she was clearly thinking about her mum.

Christmas could be a tough time of year, particularly for those who'd lost someone that they loved. He was conscious of that, and had wanted to make sure he supported her just as much as she'd supported him. But how could he do that now? She hadn't even answered any of his texts or calls.

As for his mother's behaviour? He'd been beside himself with fury. She had refused to leave Costley Hall, screaming and shouting and making demands, insulting Albert and continuing with disparaging remarks about Skye.

When Lucas had gone to try and find Skye

he'd been horrified to realise she hadn't just left the suite—but had left the entire estate.

Donald had told him he'd loaned her a car, and a tiny part of him might have been annoyed, but he knew it was entirely the right thing to do. The direct look that he'd been given by the fearless Donald had been part chastisement and part pity.

As an adult, he could see just how damaging his mother's lifestyle had been for him. It was hard for him to comprehend, because his mother was all he'd known. But most of the time there had been staff looking after him, or 'friends' who'd looked after his welfare more than she'd ever done. Getting accepted into university and moving into halls had been a relief for both of them. There had been an unwritten agreement that he wouldn't be moving back home, as he'd never really had a 'home'. And yet Costley Hall had always been here, and he'd never known it, but she had.

When he'd gone back to his suite, it had seemed that his mother had finally run out of steam.

He'd talked frankly to her, telling her exactly how much he loved Skye and what she meant to him. He'd spoken quietly, sitting at the other side of the table from her as she could hardly meet his eyes.

He'd then pushed back his anger to tell his mother how much he wished he'd known his father, and how nice it had been to meet Albert.

He could tell she was visibly stung by these words. But it was time for complete honesty between mother and son. More words had been exchanged and they'd reached an uneasy truce.

He'd wanted to tell Skye—he'd tried to tell Skye. But the last thing he'd wanted to do was to turn up uninvited at her home.

By the time he'd dealt with his patients, there was a lull in the day. Lucas spent a little time searching for Skye and finally found her in the break room, next to a lopsided Christmas tree and a mound of chocolates and biscuits. He pulled out the tin he'd been given and held it out to her.

'Olivia sent you some baking.'

Skye blinked and held out her hand, taking the tin and pulling off the lid. The smell of baking filled the room instantly.

He saw the edges of her lips hint upwards as she bent over the scones, lemon drizzle cake, tiny Christmas pudding and blackberry and apple tart.

'Wow,' she said simply.

Lucas sat down next to her. He took a deep breath.

'Can I start by telling you that Costley Hall is empty without you and I miss you more than I thought possible?'

He noticed her hand shake as she turned to look at him. There were tears in her eyes.

'Christmas Day can be hard enough. This is the first one without your mum. Am I allowed to hug you?'

Her nod was tiny. It was as if she was scared to move. So he put his arm around her shoulders and let her sink into him.

He reached over with his other hand and took hers in his, gently interlocking their fingers.

'I'm so sorry about how my mother spoke to you. And I know and appreciate you feel differently about all this, because you had a great relationship with your mum.'

Her voice came out croaky. 'But if that's how you treat your mum? What happens if things go bad between us? Will you just walk away then?'

His heart lurched. His thoughts had been

spinning. Wondering if Skye just wanted to walk in the other direction and never see him again. But these words? These words meant there was still a chance for them. And he was going to grab that with both hands—albeit a little gently.

He lifted his hand and stroked her cheek.

'Skye, I love you. We are never going to have the kind of unbalanced relationship that I have with my mother. We're equals. In this together. At least I hope we are. I spoke to her again, you know.'

'You did?' Her blue eyes met his and this time his heart squeezed inside his chest. He never wanted her to feel unsure or upset, like she clearly did now.

'Of course I did.' He sighed. 'She realised how upset I was about you leaving. I told her that I love you, and I plan to spend the rest of my life with you, and she'd better know that she'd crossed a line.'

Skye didn't say anything, just licked her lips.

'I'm always going to have a fractured relationship with my mother, Skye. But I haven't cut her off. I've restored her allowance. I've agreed we'll stay in touch. But the truth is our relationship isn't much more than that.'

Skye put her hand to her chest. 'You don't know what it feels like,' she said shakily. 'To know that you'll never have another conversation with your mum or see her again.'

He nodded. 'I get that. And you're right, I don't understand that. And maybe us talking in the last few days has cleared the air. I don't feel as resentful towards her but—' he paused for a moment '—I don't feel an overwhelming surge of love for my mother either.' He shook his head. 'I'm sad, but it's just never been there. I hear you talk about your mother, and I'm envious. I really am. I'm envious that you two were close and clearly loved each other.' He looked at her for a long moment. 'And I think that might be something we need to talk about.'

She tilted her head. 'What do you mean?'

He lowered his gaze, not wanting to upset her any further. 'You mentioned once about associating The Harlington with memories of your mum. You say you need a career change and something else to focus on. But I'm worried you're trying to run away from how you feel. Run away from the grief about your mum. And I'm worried that if we don't talk about it, you won't ever feel as if you're making the right decision, or in the place you need to be.'

She took a few minutes, clearly thinking about how things were between them.

'I've got something to tell you,' she said a little hesitantly.

His heart gave a flip-flop and he turned to face her, hoping nothing was wrong. 'What?'

She bit her bottom lip, pulled her phone from her pocket and turned it around. The screen was on her email page. 'I got three emails in the last few days, offering me all the jobs.'

'Skye, that's amazing,' he said, leaning over to give her a hug, even though his heart was immediately racing. But he quickly re-alised the hug was not reciprocated. He leaned back. 'What's wrong? Shouldn't you be celebrating?'

She nodded, and he could see the sheen in her eyes and noticed her swallow as if she had a giant lump in her throat.

'I... I...just don't know.' She gave a sad smile. 'The first person I would normally have told would have been my mum, and—' She didn't fill in the blank because she didn't need to.

He threaded his fingers through hers. 'Are

you happy about any of these jobs? Which one will you take?'

Skye was silent for a few moments, and he could see the uncertainty on her face. He hated this. A new job should make someone excited at taking on a new challenge. Although Skye was certain she was ready to make a move, would she be making the right one? And should he actually tell her he didn't want her to go anywhere? Of course he shouldn't. He had no right to do that.

She gave him the saddest smile. 'Lucas,' she said steadily, 'I need you to give me another few days. I need to sort some things out in my head.'

He swallowed, wanting to say a hundred things but knowing he had to respect her decision. And he would. Because he loved her.

He didn't want to overwhelm her. But he couldn't walk away right now without letting her know how much he cared.

'Of course,' he replied in a low voice. 'You take all the time you need. Because I'll wait,' he said with not a moment's hesitation. 'I'll wait until you're ready.'

He gave a small smile. 'Will you still do me the honour of being my date for the New Year's ball?'

This time her smile was genuine. 'I think I can manage that,' she said, then looked back down to her box of cakes. 'Now,' she said, 'I know from previous experience that you're a cake and scone stealer. So, off you go. Leave me alone to eat cake, drink tea and contemplate life.'

He squeezed her hand one more time and stood, keeping a smile on his face, even though, inside, his heart was breaking.

'You can phone me any time, day or night,' he said as he headed to the door.

Her head gave an almost imperceptible nod and he breathed in slowly and headed back out into the department, giving her the space she needed.

CHAPTER ELEVEN

AS SHE DROVE towards Costley Hall, Skye had a fluttering feeling in her chest, part excitement, part fear. She'd promised to be Lucas's date. But as she swept up the driveway she could see the estate was buzzing with people. Maybe this had been the wrong thing to agree to? There would be no chance of privacy, and Lucas would be tied up with a million responsibilities.

Olivia met her at the door with a nervous smile. 'Go on up to the Duke's suite. He's waiting for you.'

Skye was a bit out of sorts. The Christmas Day shift at the hospital had been fine, nothing too serious. When they'd finished their twelve hours at seven p.m., she'd said a brief farewell to Lucas, gone back to her place, wrapped herself in a duvet on her sofa, had a Chinese meal delivered and watched

Christmas TV. It had blocked out some of the memories that had been circulating in her head—reminding her that this was her first Christmas without any family left. It stung, not having that conversation with her mum on Christmas Day, not having something to unwrap on the day and laugh about. They'd generally always bought something fun for each other, rather than something serious. But that part of her life was gone now, and it was hard to explain to anyone.

But the run-up to New Year's Eve had been harder, and she was wondering if coming to Costley Hall was the right move. In the five years since her dad had died, Skye had always made a point of being with her mum when the clock struck twelve. This was the time of year she always had off, and they'd spent it together, sometimes at her mother's home, one time at a hotel in Scotland, and another in a resort in Tenerife. But the person she'd clinked glasses with at midnight and drank a toast to the New Year had always been her mother, and this time it was as if something dark had settled in the bottom of her stomach. She wasn't quite sure how to explain it to herself, let alone anyone else.

As she arrived at Costley Hall, she knew

deep down that part of what Lucas had said to her was right. She did need a fresh start. But she'd also been running away from her grief. A colleague had given her a card for a counsellor they'd seen when they'd lost a family member, and Skye knew it was time to pull it out and talk to someone. Maybe it would stop these feelings being so overwhelming and give her some new coping mechanisms to try. She could almost hear her mother's voice in her ear, telling her to do it. Telling her not to risk her relationship with a man that she clearly loved.

Because she did love Lucas. She knew she did. She just had to believe that he would always be willing to fight for her, like she would for him. And as she walked up the grand sweeping staircase at Costley Hall, she had to believe she was worth all this.

Today had been a whirlwind. Every time he blinked another person scooted past, preparing the Hall for the grand New Year's Eve charity ball.

Brianna, the event planner, was a wonder, her precision planning evident everywhere that Lucas looked. He had spent most of the day settling in the various children and their families from some of the charities that were represented at the ball tonight. It really was a delight to meet them all, and the whole thing did honestly feel like a family affair. Olivia was always in the background, ready to answer any questions, and Albert had been walking around looking dapper in a navy velvet jacket since just after lunchtime.

He'd barely had a chance to think all day, and that was probably for the best—because any time he did have a chance, his thoughts were fixated on Skye, hoping she would keep her promise and turn up.

When he finally got the signal from Olivia, he went quickly along to the suite, ready to meet her.

He had the biggest grin on his face as Skye walked in, a small overnight bag in her hand. A wave of relief washed over him and he moved beside her, kissing her cheek. 'I have a surprise for you,' he said.

Her nose wrinkled. 'What?'

'This,' he said, waving his hand in the direction of their bed—because that was how he thought of it, *their* bed.

Across it lay three ballgowns. One silver, one green and one a deep red. Skye let out an audible gasp and his heart lurched. She was happy. Thank goodness. He'd asked Brianna for some help, and she'd gone to town, scrolling through online stores and showing her shortlist for Lucas to have the final say.

'Where did they come from?'

'Me,' he replied with a grin. 'I got you three because I wasn't entirely sure which you'd prefer.' His heart was thudding in his chest.

Skye rolled her eyes and swung her bag onto the bed, pulling a black dress from it. She gave him a careful glance. 'I brought the one full-length gown that I actually own.' She held it up. 'It's black,' she said, 'not entirely special—' the hint of a smile was appearing on her lips '—and I bought it five years ago.' She gave him another playful glance. 'I'm not even entirely sure it still fits, but had decided to just breathe in and hope for the best.'

'If you want to wear the black dress, then you can absolutely wear whatever you like,' he said, walking over and touching the fabric, wondering if he might have overstepped.

But Skye walked over to the bed. She touched the skirt of the silver gown, which was adorned with sequins and glimmered under the lights in this room.

'All three are stunning,' she said simply.

He waited, wondering what might come next.

Her blue eyes met his. 'You make me feel like Cinderella,' she whispered.

His arms slid around her from behind. His lips near her ear, he said in a low voice, 'As long as I get to be the Prince, I can live with that.'

She spun around to face him and put her hands around his neck. 'When did you do this?'

'You know that day we were in the car, and you ordered some things?'

She nodded. 'But that was a few weeks ago, before Christmas, just when the news hit.'

He smiled in agreement. 'I know, but I asked you to the ball then, and told you to buy a ballgown.'

'But you could see that I hadn't?'

His green eyes locked with hers. 'I know you were being cautious. Even getting you to buy those beauties was a struggle.' He gestured with his head towards the parrot chaise longue and chair, which had ended up in their suite.

Skye couldn't help but beam. 'They really are magnificent in real life, aren't they?'

'If they're magnificent to you, then they're magnificent to me,' he replied with a grin.

Her head fell back as she laughed, his lips taking advantage of the bare skin at her neck.

'Hey—' she swatted him lightly with her hand '—I'm on a time limit to get ready, and so are you.' She looked at the stunning dresses again. 'I don't even know if any of these will fit yet.'

'Oh, they'll fit,' he insisted as he ran his hands up and down the curves at her waist and hips. Then he grew serious for a moment.

'How are you? I spent all Christmas night worrying about you. I wanted to phone you or text you, but you'd asked me for space so I didn't.' He gave a soft laugh. 'You have no idea how hard I found that,' he admitted.

She gave a slow nod. 'I found it hard too. I always knew the first Christmas without Mum would be like that. I thought work would distract me enough, but…' She took a deep breath, her hands resting on his shoulders. 'You might have been right about talking to someone.'

His heart squeezed for her. 'Do you know someone?'

She pressed her lips together for a moment. 'Someone at work gave me a recommendation. I think it's time to take it.'

He enveloped her in a hug. Part of him felt sorry that he'd been the person to bring this up. But he wanted her to be happy. He wanted her to feel able to move on in life and still have all the wonderful memories of her mum.

She pulled back gently. 'And how's your mum?'

Lucas contemplated the question for a second. 'Ginny is Ginny, and always will be. She's in Spain right now, celebrating New Year with friends. I've made it clear that I consider Costley Hall Albert's home, and if she wants to come and visit, she has to be courteous to him too.'

He could sense a little of the tension leave Skye's body. He reached up and twisted a bit of her hair with one of his fingers. 'You don't know how much I wish I could have had the same kind of relationship with my mum that you did with yours. But I have to accept that she is just not that kind of person and we won't have that kind of relationship. But I'll keep the door open, and I won't cut her off.'

He gave a sad smile. 'The person I'm enjoying a wonderful new relationship with is

Albert. He's an incredible man, with a wicked sense of humour and a unique experience of having to hide who he was for most of his life. I think he takes joy in recounting all the stories about my dad, and is relieved he can finally admit that they loved each other.' He led her over to the chaise lounge so they could both sit down for a moment. 'The other thing you should know is that Albert is one of your biggest fans.'

A smile broke across her face, and he knew she was flattered. 'Well, I'm kind of a fan of Albert too,' she said.

He interwove his fingers with hers. 'Did you decide what you want to do about the jobs you have been offered?' His insides felt as if they were prickling. An idea had hatched in his head, but he wasn't sure whether to mention it or not.

She shook her head and sighed. 'Not yet. I've got pros and cons for each job. All offer me a good opportunity. I've always been a nurse, I've never wanted to do anything else. But the time I had off with my mum made me want to look at other things too. I'm just not in that position really. Like the rest of the world, I need to work to pay my bills.' She sighed and looked around. 'I know that I can't *not* nurse, it's in my blood. It would just be nice to do it a little bit less?' Her final words sounded more like a question, as if she was asking what he thought.

The tiny seed that had been growing in Lucas's head started to emerge into a pink cherry blossom in full bloom. He'd watched her before at Costley Hall. The truth was, before his mother had appeared and caused a scene, it seemed that Skye fitted in even better than he did.

Maybe it was because she had no history or pressure about the place, but she seemed to excel while here. Everyone loved her. She was constantly asking questions and having conversations with the staff, finding out all she could. She was both patient and enthusiastic, and she'd made his time here easier. She'd laughed more here than in any of the time he'd known her. It had been a joy to be around her.

He knew without a doubt how he wanted things to go between them. He loved her. Skye was the first woman he'd ever connected with so much, and the fact she'd been there to share the shock and amazement about the biggest shock of his life just made them seem destined to be.

Everything about Costley Hall was a huge undertaking, and he didn't want to do it alone.

'How about doing something else?' he asked, the question making his throat dry with nerves.

'Like what?' She laughed. 'An airline pilot? A politician? A shopkeeper?'

He gulped. 'How about reducing your nursing hours and helping out at Costley Hall?'

The shock on her face was clear. He held his breath. Was this good shock, or bad?

Skye sat back in her chair and sucked in some air. 'Are you serious?'

'Of course I am. There's going to be so much to do here. I'm probably going to have to consider my hours too. I still want to be a doctor. I didn't train all these years to walk away. But...' he took a breath '... I also have to make sure that Costley Hall is run responsibly and ethically. I have the welfare of the staff to consider, and the grounds and business interests.' He shook his head. 'I can't do this alone, and I can't think of anyone I trust more.'

She sat for another few moments in stunned silence, and then slowly the edges of her lips turned upwards.

'Really?' she asked.

'Really,' he said softly. 'You must know how I feel about you.'

Her blue gaze met his. And held it. Hypnotically, as if they were both in a spell.

'No,' she said. 'Tell me.'

And this was it. The moment that he really told her how he felt. And they weren't in bed. There hadn't just been a romantic meal, or a sunset somewhere.

Lucas reached over and cupped her cheek. 'I love you,' he said tenderly, as his insides flip-flopped around about like a teenager after their first kiss. 'I love being around you, and I want to keep doing that for a very long time.'

Tears flooded into her eyes. She reached up her hand to cover his on her cheek, then dipped her head for a few moments, catching her breath. When she lifted her head again, she was smiling.

'I feel the same,' she said. 'It feels like you appeared at just the right time, to take my mind from other things, and fill a giant gap in my life.'

'Well, I'm glad I was convenient,' he joked.

Her hand clenched his. 'Oh, you're not convenient, Lucas Hastings.' She raised her eyebrows. 'In fact, you're anything but convenient. You've been quite troublesome, actually. It's just as well I think you're handsome, smart and worth the bother.'

She leaned over and kissed him quickly, pulling back in case anyone else might see.

'I'd love to have a role at Costley Hall,' she said, looking thoughtful. 'I do like it here. And I do like the people, and maybe this is the change I need to make in my life.' She took a breath. 'I've always been so self-sufficient that reducing my hours might feel strange for me.'

'You mean, as in your salary?'

She nodded. 'It pays my rent, my bills, for everything. I like the fact that I can make my own way in life.'

He understood what she meant. 'But if you take the job at the GP practice close to here, it would make more sense to live at Costley Hall. It's much closer. You could give up your rental. And don't think you won't get paid for what you do at Costley Hall—of course you will. You're not going to lose any of your income.'

He could say more. He could say that he'd quite happily offer her much more than that, but he wanted to wait for the perfect moment.

Skye looked thoughtful for a few seconds,

then gave a nod, a warm-hearted smile on her face. 'I like the sound of that,' she whispered.

His nose brushed the side of her cheek. 'I like the sound of that too,' he whispered. 'Now, let's get changed. We've got a ball to attend.'

CHAPTER TWELVE

IF SOMEONE HAD told her at the beginning of this year that two of the biggest events of her life would happen, she wouldn't have believed them. But the saddest and happiest parts of her life were coming together.

She ducked into the bathroom and quickly showered, finding appropriate underwear and quickly pulling on each dress in turn. They were all stunning but the silver dress gave her a different kind of sensation—like she could rule the world.

It wasn't a traditional, sticky-out ballgown. It had small cap sleeves, a slightly plunging heart-shaped neckline, then skimmed her hips in a shimmer of silver sequins until it hit the floor. A pair of strappy silver sandals matched it perfectly and by the time she'd applied her make-up, her heart was beating in anticipation.

Was this how it might feel to be lady of the manor, so to speak? She took a few moments, sitting in her parrot chair and running her hand over the velvet, admiring the bright reds, greens and yellows of the parrots on the dark blue material. It was as if someone had flipped a switch and turned her life into something else.

Did she, Skye Carter, really deserve all this?

She closed her eyes and tried to imagine telling her mum about all this, and how happy she would have been to meet Lucas and see the impact he'd had on Skye's life.

She stood up, finding renewed confidence. As she made her way to the top of the stairs she could see Lucas, dressed in his suit, waiting for her. It felt as if her grin was too wide for her face as he slid his arm around her waist.

'Ready to greet our guests?'

Butterflies were in her stomach, but as she looked down into the foyer where their guests were gathering, removing their jackets and getting some refreshments, she could feel the buzz in the air.

The doors were open to the main ballroom,

with its bright twinkling chandeliers and gold and silver decorations.

'A couple of months ago, I was just a doctor,' said Lucas, and she could hear the hint of nerves in his voice.

She put her hand on his chest. 'Lucas Hastings, you've never been *just* a doctor.' She gave him an understanding look. 'But now you're also the Duke of Mercia, and you're going to be wonderful. And tonight will be perfect.'

He kissed her cheek and they descended the stairs together and Skye breathed out, letting the tension she was feeling release throughout her body.

Tonight would be wonderful. And, with Lucas's hand in hers, this place was starting to feel real. Starting to feel like it could be home.

The countdown had begun. Brianna had assembled the crowd from the ballroom at the bottom of the stairs, and even though it seemed as if the eyes of the world were on him, Lucas was finally beginning to feel comfortable in this newly shaped Duke-sized skin.

And he was quite sure the reason he could feel confident about this was because of the woman by his side.

Skye really had no idea how natural she was at all this. Maybe it was the years of experience as a nurse, her ability to read people and assess a situation. But each person she met with ease. There were some people here tonight who were impossibly rich—like he was—but they had clearly never seen, or understood, need or poverty.

There were others from some of the charities who were in treatment, needed support or came from some of the most deprived parts of the country. Lucas was realising how far his father's reach had been, and how he'd worked hard not to think only of his privilege. There were also some staff here to share in the festivities, and some local business owners and people from the nearby village.

There were also a few members of the press. Lucas had baulked at this, but Brianna had reassured him that good press was necessary for the charities and their continued funding. And she'd smiled sweetly and told him he just had to suck it up. She'd patted his shoulder and given him a fond look.

'You're just like your father,' she'd said, and for the first time he'd felt a little pride.

He slipped his arm around Skye's waist as she stood next to him at the top of the stairs.

'You look stunning,' he whispered, dropping a kiss on her cheek. 'And you've been the perfect hostess.'

'I'm learning,' she said with a smile on her face as she looked at the crowd beneath them, and he could feel her tremble slightly.

He raised his glass to the people below as Brianna flicked a switch to flash the lights to get everyone's attention. A few hundred people stopped talking and stared up at him expectantly.

'Thank you everyone for coming this evening. You all know that this is my first official duty as the Duke of Mercia.' A few people whistled and clapped at his use of his title and Lucas smiled.

'It's no secret that this has all been a surprise for me, but I've spent the last few weeks learning about the work my father did at Costley Hall and for the various charities he supported.'

Again, there were a few cheers.

'So, even though I'm new at all this, I want you to know that I'm keen to continue the good work my father did, working with local businesses and supporting all the charities that were dear to his heart.'

From the corner of his eye he glimpsed the

navy smoking jacket of Albert, and the early lift of his glass in support.

'I ask for your patience as I learn this new role, and I will be continuing my work as a doctor.' He turned to Skye. 'I want to start this New Year a little differently from how my father used to do things.' He took a few deep breaths. 'The last few weeks, as I've learned of my new role, and come to terms with what it will mean to be a duke, I have been lucky enough to have someone by my side. Someone I consider to be my best friend.'

Skye's eyes widened, and his smile broadened.

'So, I want to start the New Year by taking a very important step. This job is bigger than one person. Probably even bigger than two, but we'll get to that in time.'

Skye's mouth opened and the crowd cheered.

Lucas put his hand over his heart. 'I've met the person who makes me whole. The person who gives me perspective when I need it, and who has my back. She's the first person I think about in the morning, and the last person I think about at night. I think I'm probably the luckiest man alive that I started work at The Harlington and got to meet the feisty, no-nonsense charge nurse that worked there.'

He dropped down onto one knee and pulled the box from his pocket that he'd taken from the safe earlier.

Skye's hands covered her mouth.

'Skye Carter, I love you with my whole heart. I've never felt connected with someone the way I do with you. I promise to always love you, now and for ever. Will you do me the honour of being my wife?'

The crowd held its breath, along with Lucas, as he waited for his answer. He'd flipped open the black velvet box to reveal the ring he'd found in the family safe earlier. It was a family heirloom. A large single diamond set in yellow gold. He'd worried Skye might find it old-fashioned, or it might not be to her taste. But Albert, his co-conspirator, had told him it didn't matter and he could let her pick what she wanted later. But if he was going to ask the question, he had to have a ring.

Skye finally dropped her hands from her face. Her eyes glittered with tears.

'Yes,' she whispered.

He took the ring from the box, conscious that the crowd below hadn't heard. But as he slid the ring onto her finger, the crowd gave a cheer as he took Skye in his arms.

'You've made me so happy,' he said in a low voice.

Her hand rested on his chest. 'You've made me happy too,' she replied. 'More than you could ever know.'

Lucas glanced at the large clock above the entranceway. He picked up some glasses of champagne that were sitting nearby. 'What's a duke without a duchess?' he shouted jubilantly, and the crowd laughed and cheered again, lifting their glasses to them.

He slid one arm around Skye as he looked down at all the people watching them. He should be nervous, maybe even a little overwhelmed. But he wasn't. And that was because he had Skye by his side.

'Let's have a countdown to the New Year.' He raised his glass, and started counting. 'Ten, nine...'

The crowd beneath him joined in, and he looked into Skye's eyes as they said the last few numbers together, dropping a kiss on her red lips as they reached one.

'Duchess?' she murmured under her breath. 'I hadn't even thought about that.'

He smiled, their lips only millimetres apart and their foreheads touching. 'Sounds kinda nice, doesn't it? How are we going to top this of people even if they were no longer working in a hospital environment.

'And if I didn't have the resources to make all of these things happen?'

She understood why he was so cautious, not knowing for sure whether his family status had influenced her decision to be with him because of his experience with his ex.

Soraya took his head in her hands. 'I love you, Raed. I don't care if you're a prince, or a surgeon, or a paper boy. I want to be with you.'

He nodded. 'So you'll marry me, then?'

The question shocked her. They hadn't talked about marriage again since she'd moved over, and she'd thought it was something he would only consider further down the line when their future out here was more secure.

'I mean, I considered the full romance package for the proposal, roses, champagne, down on one knee...but we did all that and it didn't work out so well first time around.'

'Yes.' The answer slipped easily from her lips. 'I'll marry you, Raed. Right now if we could. I love you.'

'I love you too, Princess.'

He smiled and it was better than anything money could buy. He was right. They didn't need all the bells and whistles to prove their love for one another, they just needed each other.

Money and status didn't mean anything as long as they had love.

* * * * *

*Look out for the next story in
the Royal Docs duet*

A Mother for His Little Princess

*And if you enjoyed this story, check out
these other great reads from Karin Baine*

Nurse's Risk with the Rebel
Falling Again for the Surgeon
Single Dad for the Heart Doctor

All available now!